KIRK'S LAW

Books by Robert Newton Peck

A DAY NO PIGS WOULD DIE

PATH OF HUNTERS

MILLIE'S BOY

SOUP

FAWN

WILD CAT

BEE TREE (poems)

SOUP AND ME

HAMILTON

HANG FOR TREASON

RABBITS AND REDCOATS

KING OF KAZOO (a musical)

TRIG

LAST SUNDAY

THE KING'S IRON

PATOOIE

SOUP FOR PRESIDENT

EAGLE FUR

TRIG SEES RED

BASKET CASE

HUB

MR. LITTLE

CLUNIE

SOUP'S DRUM

SECRETS OF
   SUCCESSFUL FICTION

TRIG GOES APE

SOUP ON WHEELS

JUSTICE LION

TRIG OR TREAT

KIRK'S LAW

KIRK'S LAW

Robert Newton Peck

DOUBLEDAY & COMPANY, INC.
GARDEN CITY, NEW YORK

Library of Congress Cataloging in Publication Data

Peck, Robert Newton.
Kirk's law.

SUMMARY: A rugged life-style in the Vermont woods
with a fiesty old hunter called Wishbone Kirk
develops the character of a 15-year-old boy.
[1. Vermont—Fiction] I. Title.
PZ7.P339Kk   [Fic]
ISBN: 0-385-17242-7 Trade
ISBN: 0-385-17243-5 Prebound
Library of Congress Catalog Card Number 80-2058

KIRK'S LAW

1

"Are we lost?"

"Not hopelessly, son. Actually I'm hoping that we're headed into better days."

As he spoke, my father didn't look at me, but kept his eyes on the dirt road. He'd been driving uphill, winding into the mountains for close to an hour. The big Lincoln seemed impatient to get wherever it was we were going.

"I give up, Dad. Where are we?"

"There's a map of Vermont in the glove compartment. If you want to know something, son, look it up. And if you don't want to ever learn anything, then there's always the alternative."

"What's that?"

"You'll be one moment closer to growing up a loser."

I sighed. To avoid one more of his boring lectures on my character, I reached into the glove box, got out the map, and unfolded it. Earlier, we had driven through the town of Middlebury, and we were continuing north.

"Where's the school?"

"There isn't one, Collin. At least not in the sense of your question. You're not going to a school."

"But you said—"

"If you'll recall, I told you that you were to be enrolled at a place where you might finally learn something. Neither your mother nor I ever mentioned the word *school*."

My body stiffened against the car seat, afraid to ask the next question. He was dumping me somewhere in this wilderness of trees. Looking out the window, I saw white patches of early April snow. Cold and alone.

"I have a right to know where you're taking me."

"Yes, you do. And so I'll tell you."

"Okay."

Visions of a reform school or a mental hospital flashed through my brain. So far I hadn't been sent to either one. Yet maybe it was only a matter of time.

"You are en route to an education that I hope will sink in, one that you'll appreciate far more than just another costly prep academy for you to get bounced out of."

"I'm sorry about all that. Honest."

"You didn't do well in public school, so I sent you to Kent last fall. With your solemn promise that you'd do better there."

"I know." As I spoke, my hands wanted to crumple the map I was holding.

"You read the letter, Collin. Your grades were poor, your conduct ungentlemanly, plus the fact that I doubt you made even one friend."

What my father was saying was true. School was a drag, no matter where. But maybe the mystery now ahead of me would be worse.

"Your life has been too cozy, Collin. It's been a feather bed. And because of that, you're becoming flabby in body and spirit."

My stomach felt sick. I wanted him to shut up, turn the car around, and take us back to Connecticut. Okay, I might even have another go at Greenwich High School. At least there were some foxy girls there. And a few sharp guys who knew the score.

"What am I going to study?"

"Law."

"You mean it's a law school?"

"In a way, yes. But not at all like Harvard or Yale. However, you'll learn more law from the teacher I've selected for you than you ever could from briefing cases."

"I won't stay up here in this hog hole."

"Oh, so you already plan to jump ship before you even judge the place or meet the headmaster."

"Maybe."

"Maybe, you say? Well, maybe I've been a delinquent father. I know I haven't had much influence on you. Your interests are little more than television, junk food, loud music, dirty movies, and bubble-gum girls that dress like teen-age hookers."

"I have a right to have fun."

"Yes, you do. Every person has rights. And more, to defend those rights is a duty. Without duty and dedication, rights have a way of melting. Without a cold winter, ice softens."

"So?" I used the word that annoyed him.

"So—what I am going to serve you, dear son, is a helping of cold winter. And are you ever due for one."

"It's April."

"True. But your winter, Collin, is about to begin. The hardest and toughest winter of your life."

"Why are you doing this to me? To get even? Because I got my fanny kicked out of Kent—and you won't get your precious money back."

"I care about the money, yes. But, oddly enough, I care more about Collin Pepper."

"That's a laugh."

"No, it's not a laugh. But it is why I'm forcing you into a winter of work. Hopefully, then, you'll appreciate your springtime, when it finally dawns."

"I don't get it."

"You will."

"This place you're dragging me to—is it some sort of reform school or prison?"

"Not a prison. But I'm banking on its being the

toughest reform school, in a manner of speaking, that a fifteen-year-old boy ever attended."

I wanted to cry. Yet I'd be damned if I'd give him the joy of watching me do it. To hell with my father, with Greenwich, with Kent and every other school in the world.

"I'll run away. You can't make me hibernate up here in this crummy hole. It's the pits."

"Perhaps you'll find the fortitude to stay and tough it out."

"No way."

"If you cut loose and run, where will you go? For a while, you will *not* be allowed to come home. I forbid it."

"Does Mom know you're doing all this?"

"She knows. I confess she likes the idea even less than you do. But I convinced her that we'd give it a whirl."

I wanted to chop his face. Or grab the wheel and wreck the car. That would fix the big jerk, to see his precious Lincoln in a ditch with the radiator steaming, and no tow truck. No handy Linc-Merc dealer to do his dirty work.

I pulled out my comb and ran it through my hair. I knew that seeing me do that always bugged him. He was bald. Sure enough, he popped off on cue.

"I've raised a boy who thinks more about his hair than he does about his character. I truly hope, Collin, that your values will soon strengthen."

"In prison?"

"Quite the contrary. Freedom is a strength of soul. It has little to do with confinement."

"Big joke."

"You may become more of a free man up here than you ever imagined."

"Yeah, fat chance."

"And it is not a penitentiary. If you feel you're in prison, as so many kids your age consider family life, then you are locked behind bars that you have built yourself. Bars harder than steel."

"You're just lipping all that bull."

"Not really. And I hope you'll realize I'm not putting you into a jail up here. I'm really trying to release you from your own little miserable cell."

"You sure have a shifty way of turning everything around, Dad."

"Do I?"

"Yeah."

"Well, now it's going to be your turn."

"To do what?"

"To turn *yourself* around. Collin, you're my son. But a boy doesn't belong to his parents. We don't own you."

"Who does?"

"You do. Adulthood is owning one's self, and not becoming a serf to others. But more than that—and this perhaps is a bit subtle—never being a slave to one's own weakness."

"You think I'm a weakling. You always have."

"No. But I believe that inside everyone abide a weakling and a hero. The base and the lofty."

"I don't want to be a hero. All I want is to have some fun. And not have to hear somebody bug me every five minutes. You want me to be like you, a big-wheel businessman. I'm not. So you hate my guts."

"This trip to Vermont, son, is not for me to hate you."

"What's it for?"

"It's for you to start liking yourself."

2

"We're here."

I shrugged. We're where? All I saw ahead of the car was where the dirt road became what appeared to be little more than a pair of wagon ruts. Covered with pine needles. Two brown trails that led upward to nothing but trees. Not a soul in sight.

Dad saw me shiver. "Don't be afraid. You're not going to be horsewhipped. Show some guts."

"I want to go home."

"Collin, you've *been* home. All your life, except for six months at Kent. Did you ever stoop down and pull a weed, or wash a dish, or help me clean out the garage on Saturday? Hardly ever, unless I threatened to banish you to your room, which you turned into a pigsty."

"I like home. Honest."

"Perhaps you will a year from now. Get out of the car, please."

We got out.

"What is this place? Is it some sort of a penal camp you read about in the *Times?*"

"You'll find out." My father opened the trunk. "Haul out your gear. We're hiking from here on."

I'd brought two suitcases and a bedroll, plus, at my mother's suggestion, a small box of books, most of which I'd never bothered to read.

"Aren't you going to help me?"

"No."

"All this stuff weighs a ton."

My father scowled. "Tough."

Loading myself like a pack mule, I followed Dad up the path. No ordinary car could have been driven here. Each of the two ruts contained rocks that jutted up from the hard earth, bigger than dead turtles.

"How much farther?"

"Keep moving. We're almost there."

Almost where? I was starting to pant, and my arms ached. I was thinking of the day that Dad and Mom had taken me to Kent and helped me trim up my room. Mom had even lined the bottoms of my bureau drawers with white paper. And sorted out my socks and underwear. Then she'd made up my bed.

Josh Witten, my new roommate, had looked on as she did all that. Then, after Mom and Dad kissed me good-bye and left, Witten had looked at me for a long time. Finally he spoke.

"Pepper, you're a candy-ass."

No wonder, I was thinking as I stumbled along after Dad, that I'd hated Kent. I had to room with

that gung ho jock who wanted to be another Bruce
Jenner.

"Wait up, Dad."

Ahead of me, he was hiking faster than I could
trot. Stopping, I changed hands on the bigger of the
two suitcases. But it didn't help. My fingers hurt.

I heard his voice. "Come along."

Rounding a bend in the trail, I saw what I figured
was our destination. And it was a dump. I didn't
know what to expect, but this wasn't it. Just a grubby
old shack in a clearing of pines.

Was he going to leave me here alone?

My eyes burned. Yet if I blinked, the fright would
roll down my face, and I didn't want Dad to see that.
Candy-ass! I wanted to go back to Kent and punch
out Josh Witten. Even though I knew he could eat
my lunch with one fist.

"Is this it?"

Dad nodded. "Yes."

"Do I stay here?"

"For a while."

"Alone?"

"No. You'll be meeting the boss."

Boss? The word stung me. But it didn't look to
me as if anyone was there, except for Dad and me.

My father yelled. "Hello!"

A dog barked. Not from inside the shack, but from
beyond us, in the woods. I thought I heard a human
voice order the dog to be still.

Looking around, I saw an old man.

"Howdy," he said.

He was bowlegged, as if riding an unseen horse. The clothes he wore seemed to be all of one color, like the earth. Even the dog was a grayish brown, as though the pair of them had been stirred and poured from the same batch of wool and fur.

"How are you, Mr. Kirk?" said my dad.

"Tolerable. See you made it."

Dad and the old man shook hands while I stood in my tracks, without even dropping my gear. Slowly I set my stuff on the ground. I wanted to run.

"Mr. Kirk, I'd like you to meet my son, Collin Pepper."

I didn't know quite what to do, or how to do it. Both the old man and the dog were watching me, waiting for me to make the first move. The dog didn't growl or wag its tail. But it looked at me with intelligent eyes, as if already knowing who I was and why I was here. Things I didn't know.

I stumbled forward to extend my hand to the old man. "How do you do, sir."

The hand that suddenly gripped mine was far stronger than I had anticipated. Sort of like locking claws with a lion.

The old man's eyes looked deeply into mine, as if searching for some clue to prove that I was Anthony Pepper's boy. His handshake pumped up and down, just once. As he released my hand, I wanted to wash it. Yet he didn't look or smell dirty.

"So this is your son, Mr. Pepper."

"That he is."

"Good. This here is Tool. Don't pet her just yet, boy. She's a bit distant on strangers."

I had no intention of petting that dog. Not today and not ever.

"Smell him, girl."

Tool moved slowly toward me, while I froze. She wasn't a big dog, but she looked tough—lean and rangy. I could count her ribs. Her jaw muscles flexed as she slowly sniffed my pants legs, shoes, and then my hand, which I lifted up and away from her snout.

"Don't shy, boy. She'll come to you and whiff you out. Let your hand hang loose and easy."

Closing my eyes, I let Tool inhale whatever it was she was curious over.

"Back."

At the one-word command, Tool returned to the old man's side, sat, and watched me. I would not have wanted to start trouble with Mr. Kirk. Anyone who did, I was thinking, would no longer have a throat.

"You boys hungry?"

Dad smiled my way. "Are we, Collin?"

"Yes, sir," I said to Mr. Kirk. "We sure are."

I figured it was the thing to say, even though the idea of food prepared inside that shack wasn't too appetizing. Hours ago, Dad and I had stopped at a diner in northern Connecticut and eaten breakfast. The sausages came up in my mouth.

"Come on in."

Tool stayed outside the door as the three of us entered the tiny shack. There was only one cot, covered with an olive-drab blanket marked U. S. Army. No pillow. One chair, a black rocker with worn arms. I noticed a big black stove, almost the size of a horse, which bore raised letters on its flank that read Acme American.

"Take a seat."

Dad sat in the rocker, and I helped myself to the foot of the cot. The springs whined as I sat.

"Stew," said Mr. Kirk. "Only take a moment to heat up. Then we'll do our food."

"Your place looks the same," my father said.

It didn't take much figuring to decide that he'd been in here before. I wanted to ask when, but Dad answered my question.

"I met Mr. Kirk before you were born. Years before, when some other men and I came up here to fish one May. In trout season."

"That's nice," I said. It sounded kind of dumb, but I didn't know what else to say. Nor did I care.

"He was our guide. And over the seasons, we became friends."

"Oh."

"And now, faced with this big problem in my life, I truly believe the best friend I have on earth is Wishbone Kirk."

3

"Good luck, Collin."

We had been here little more than an hour when my father said he was leaving. Even as I heard him say it, I couldn't seem to react. It was as if I was in shock. Nothing seemed to matter. I felt numb.

"I'll let you and Mr. Kirk get acquainted on your own. That way you can decide what kind of man he is, and also discover the kind of boy you are."

My father and I were alone, by the Lincoln. The old man and the dog had stayed back at the shack.

"I hate this stinking hole."

"You do now. Maybe you'll change your mind."

"Never. And you can't make me stay here."

"No, I can't. I've done all I can for you today, Collin. From now on, your life and how you live it is in your hands. I'll let you determine if Mr. Kirk is a gentleman worth knowing."

"You want his opinion of me, is that it?"

"No, strangely I don't. What matters is not your opinions of each other, but your opinion of yourself."

"I won't stay. I'll split."

"That's all up to you, son. There are no fences."

He held out his hand, but I ignored it. Instead, I just turned my back and walked up the trail, stopping only when I heard him start the Lincoln and then drive away into stillness. Leaning against a tree, I closed my eyes and, with cold fingers, ripped away fragments of the shaggy bark. God, how I hated my father.

I felt chilly. April was supposed to be warm, like springtime. But this was early April in Vermont. There was still snow in the woods under the trees. And the bare ground felt hard and mean.

I was determined not to cry. I thought, I'll be damned if I'll be a candy-ass kid, and it isn't because I give a hoot what Kirk thinks. The old coot probably can't think at all. Who needs a brain up on a mountain? There's nothing or no one here to think about.

Tool barked.

Opening my eyes, I saw her above me on the trail. Trotting in my direction, she passed me, turned, and barked at me twice more. It was clear she intended me to take one route, the route back to the shack.

Was I to take orders from a dog? As if in answer, she growled lightly, her eyes leaving me to look up the trail. This rotten dog was no fool. And not a beast to mess with. Her deeper growl warned me that she meant business. So I walked very slowly in front of her. The old man stood waiting for us just outside his cabin.

"I sent Tool to fetch you."

"Sure." I nodded to Mr. Kirk.

"Remember, don't reach out to touch her or pet her. And don't raise your voice when she's nearby. Understood?"

"Yes, I understand."

"Done."

The old man sat down on one end of a fallen log, looking at me. His eyes were very blue. And clear. As though he could look through a stone wall to see what hid beyond. In a way, his eyes were intelligent, like Tool's.

"Your name is Collin."

"Collin Richardson Pepper."

"Well, mine's Sabbath. I guess it was my ma's idea. *Sabbath* means *Sunday*, and *Kirk* means *church*. Sabbath Kirk. Folks don't use it much."

"Why not?"

"Sit down and I'll tell you."

I sat at the other end of the log, straddling it like a wooden horse.

"Because of my bandy legs, folks started calling me Wishbone. And I don't favor that much either."

"I see." I wasn't going to smile at him or be interested in any of his dumb, boring stories.

The old man fumbled in the pocket of his jacket

and produced a pipe. It was a yellow bowl, sort of like a corncob. Unrolling a package of tobacco, he stuffed the pipe and lit it with six puffs.

"Do you smoke?"

I'd tried menthol cigarettes and a cigar, along with a joint that had made me sick and dried out my mouth and throat. Smoking was a waste of time and money.

"No, I don't." I wanted to tell him that it wasn't any of his business.

"Good. The woods are wet now. But they'll rustle dry soon as May."

"Yes, I suppose so." I should have said more, to impress him that I wasn't an old Vermont red-neck like himself, but rather a sharp dude from Greenwich.

"So, here we be, boy. Thee and me. You reckon we'll make her do, or dasn't?"

"I don't care."

"Up here, we're more than a hog call from what's called civilization. We're alone. You and me and old Tool here. Best we get on."

"I guess."

"You're a quiet gent. I'll give you that. Well, is there anything you want to know?"

"Yes, there is."

"Then ask."

"Is my father paying you for keeping me here? If he is, I want to know, seeing as it's our money. How much?"

Mr. Kirk squinted his eyes at me, crinkling his face into doubt. Before answering, he reached over to stroke Tool's head.

"No, he ain't paid me a lick."

"How come?"

"Your pa offered, but I wouldn't take it. Not a penny. Truth is, I intend to pay you."

"You're going to pay *me*?"

"Right."

"For what?"

"For hard work. Six full days a week. Tool and I rest on Sunday. Us two and the Lord Almighty."

"I want to know what kind of work and how much I'll be paid. Maybe it's work I don't know how to do."

"Maybe so, and maybe no. You think you can tackle the job?"

Right then, I decided there wasn't anything in the world that this moth-eaten relic could beat me at. Besides, I didn't have one cent in my pocket. Not a penny or a watch to pawn. So maybe I could earn enough to run away on.

I said, "You name it."

"Ha! That's the spirit."

I decided this old geezer might be easier to fool than I'd imagined. Easy, because he no doubt liked my father. And I was Anthony Pepper's boy. People believe what they want to believe. I smiled. It would be a snap to get the old guy to eat out of my hand. And if the work was too tough, I'd just play sick.

Work myself up into a fever by holding my hands in hot water. My mother fell for that trick more than once. And she's a lot smarter than Kirk.

"Okay, so I get paid wages."

"Wrong, boy. You earn wages."

"How much?"

"Dollar a month. If'n you prove out worthy."

I smiled to fool him into thinking I was kidding. "And what if I don't work?"

"Then you don't get paid a wage."

"Fair enough."

"And no food."

4

"Let's have at it."

I didn't know what he meant. Mr. Kirk stood up quickly, knocking the black and gray ashes from the bowl of his pipe. He stuck the pipe into his jacket.

"Time to go to work."

I sighed—a big mistake, as the old man caught me doing it and squinted at me. His look made me wonder how much my father had told him about me and how lazy I was. Yet I had a feeling that Mr. Kirk was a person who would make up his own mind and not rely on someone else's opinion.

"Where are we going?"

"Hunting."

"For what?"

"Food."

I'd asked a dumb question. So maybe his answer wasn't meant to be as abrupt as it sounded.

He went inside the shack and reappeared in less than half a minute, carrying a gun in the crook of his arm. Noticing the gun, Tool leaped into the air three or four times, her tail busy.

"What kind of gun is that?"

"It's a Purdey."

"A rifle?"

"Shotgun. Sixteen gauge."

"Is it loaded?"

"Nope."

Reaching into his pocket, Mr. Kirk pulled out a red shell with a gold cap. He broke open the gun, loaded it, and snapped it shut with a sharp click. Then with his thumb, he twisted the release, broke open the gun again, and extracted the shell.

"Understand?"

"I think so."

"Do it."

The gun weighed heavy in my hands. But after a brief fumble, I installed the shell and removed it. Then I handed both to the old man. It was his gun, not mine. He refused the gun and took only the shell.

"You tote it."

"Okay."

"Carry a gun with the barrel down, be it at load or unload. And never walk behind another man if you tote a firearm."

"What about the dog?"

"Tool knows. She'll follow me, not you. I'll trail behind you, and she'll shadow. I don't guess you'll need tell *her* much about hunting. If we look and listen, she'll tell us."

"Which way?"

The old man nodded. "North, toward the lake."

I expected to see several paths leading to and away from the shack, but there were none. There just didn't seem to be any particular route to follow.

"You don't have a path."

"No."

"How come?"

"Because when I'm in the woods, I always approach my cabin by a different direction. Not many strangers will find us unless they happen to stagger into my clearing."

Was he hiding? Mr. Kirk didn't seem too anxious to meet the outside world.

"Go north."

"Which way is that?"

"Look at the sun. Then march according."

Well, I'd take a stab at it. I walked with the afternoon sun occasionally hitting the back of my left shoulder. The old man said nothing, so I figured I was correctly pointed.

The woods I headed into were not brushy but open. Over our heads, the rustling pines were green high up. Under our feet was nothing but a fawn carpet of needles, soft and silent.

"Whoa."

Hearing his one word, I turned around. The gun pivoted with me until it aimed at his belly. Almost before I realized what I'd done, he dodged, grabbed the barrel, and yanked—and I felt its butt ram into my stomach.

I grunted.

"Never," he said.

So I'd done a stupid thing. Turned carelessly around and pointed a shotgun at the man behind me. It made me feel like a fool.

"*You* turn. The gun don't."

"Damn it." My belly hurt, and I glowered at Mr. Kirk to let him know it.

"Which is worse, boy? My poke in your gut or you blowing my head off?"

I didn't answer him. One would heal and one wouldn't, so I guess I didn't have a smart-mouth answer. But he had poked me a lot harder than necessary. The gun butt had punched me slightly below the rib cage, and I felt deflated in two ways. But I'd get even.

"North," grunted Kirk.

Saying nothing, I kept walking, aware once more of the sun on my left shoulder, behind me. He sure was a sour old coot. Maybe he'd let me load the gun again, and then I'd give him the fright of his worthless life. Not kill him or wound him. Maybe just pull the trigger and miss him by inches. Pretend it was accidental. Or shoot his dumb dog.

If Kirk was going to become ornery, I'd show him how mean Collin Pepper could get. Thinking about it didn't make me feel so hot. Well, maybe I'd forgive him. Just this once.

"Boy?"

I didn't stop, but only slowed my pace a bit, wondering what the old man wanted to tell me. Probably another dumb order.

"I regret the hurt of it. But it's a rule to remember. Here, take this."

This time I stopped and turned halfway around with my upper body, making sure the Purdey was aimed ahead of me. Mr. Kirk held out a small green leaf, about an inch long, shaped like a tiny football.

"Chew it."

"What is it?" If the guy was trying to poison me, I wasn't going to be a pushover.

"Wintergreen."

Mr. Kirk popped a leaf just like it into his own mouth and chewed. So I took it and bit down. The leaf was hard, but its flavor was something like a weak Life Saver.

"Not bad. Is it real wintergreen?"

"Yup."

"Thanks."

"It'll ease that sore middle of yours. And maybe even that sore temper."

I stopped chewing, sorry I had bothered to thank him. Tool slowly moved to stand between us. Her eyes never left me.

"Temper," the old man said, "ain't useful. But your head is, if'n you work it right."

I nodded.

"Now then, is your temper cool enough to load the Purdey?"

"Yes."

He handed me a red shell, and I locked it into the shotgun. "There's nothing to shoot at."

"See that stump?"

"Where?"

"Right yonder." He pointed. "There's a nub on the up side, to the left. Blow it away."

Raising the gun to my shoulder, I sighted along the barrel, pretending that I was used to guns and knew what I was doing.

"Hug it hard, lad. Rest your cheek to the stock and let you and the gun be of one bone. All of a piece."

"I know."

Sighting at the nub, I closed my eyes and pulled the trigger. The roar and the recoil made me feel as if I'd shot myself. And the smell was sour. The nub atop the rotted stump was still there. How could I have missed with a shotgun?

"Trigger squeeze," said the old man.

"But I did."

"No, you yanked it. Reload. And this time, squeeze it gentle, so that the report of the gun comes as a surprise. Hold your sight picture steady—that's right—and always squeeze off slow and easy at a stone-still target."

The gun barked. I hit the nub, exploding the wood into a spray of reddish-brown fragments.

"Wow!"

"Good shot. Maybe you'll be a hunter."

"It's easy. A real breeze."

Mr. Kirk squinted at me. "Ever killed an animal?"

"No."

"Well, that ain't so easy. Stumps don't bleed."

5

"Hark."

I stopped, wondering what had captured the old man's attention. "Did you hear something?" I whispered.

"Nope. But Tool's got a scent."

Her tail whipped one way after another. Nose to the ground, she trotted off, and Mr. Kirk nudged me to follow. He stayed close behind me.

"What are we after up here?"

"You'll see."

"Deer?"

"Nope. Not after the racket we made a while back. Won't be no deer within a day's walk of where we stand. Long gone."

"Okay, but—"

"Besides, we got scatter load in them shells. Buck load is a slug. One lead ball. Savvy?"

I nodded. "But didn't we shoo off all the game when I was practicing?"

"Some. Animals vary. Some got memories, and others forget real quick. We'll just ease along behind Tool and let her work the supper back to us."

"What'll we do?"

"Sit."

We sat with our backs to pines, our knees upraised. I made sure the muzzle of the loaded Purdey pointed away from its owner.

"When the time comes, boy, please don't shoot the dog."

"I'll be careful. Wasn't I pretty good in practice? I hit what you told me to shoot at."

"You hit it."

Tool barked. The noise sounded as if she were a mile away, though it was hard to be sure up here in the woods. It wasn't much like Greenwich, Connecticut.

I was trying not to think about home and Mom, and making an effort to forget the dismal sound that Dad's car made when he was driving away. Leaving me here. And on my first day I could have killed the old man by accident. Or maybe even on purpose. What kind of a kid was I anyhow? Maybe I really was crazy.

My mind wandered. Chewing wintergreen sure isn't much of a turn-on, I thought. I suppose it's the biggest thrill in old Kirk's life, though, munching on a little leaf. I bet he's never been anywhere, or even heard of New York. Lives alone. And no woman? Maybe the old guy's nuts. How could any person stay sane up here in a Vermont wilderness all by himself? Well, he has Tool.

We have Winnie. She was supposed to be my dog, but she never really liked me very much. Winnie was always Mom's dog. Mom never goes to the kitchen that Win doesn't pad along behind her.

Winnie the Poodle. Boy, what a dumb name. Maybe it fits a dog that hardly ever goes out of the house. Mostly she goes on the carpet. I'm glad Mom cleans it up. Winnie wouldn't like it up here either. You can bet that Tool would look at her the same way the old man looks at me. At least I can't mess on Kirk's carpet. He doesn't have any. Only boards.

I looked at Mr. Kirk. Was he sleeping? His eyes were closed as he leaned back against the trunk of a big pine.

"Are you asleep?"

"Nope. Just listening."

"There isn't anything to hear."

"Try it with your eyes shut."

I closed my eyes and listened. Birds. Not nearby, but off somewhere in the treetops. Little flocks of chirping that came from all over.

"What are they?"

"Chickadees."

"I don't see any."

"You won't. They probable see us. And hear us."

"What color are they? Like sparrows?"

"Nope. Sparrows be brown. A chickadee is black, gray, and white."

"The kind they put on Christmas cards?"

"I 'spect so. Don't know for certain. Nobody ever mailed me one, except your pa."

"Dad sent you a Christmas card?"

"Every year. It's the only one I get."

"Do you send him one?"

"Nope."

"How do you get your mail?"

"In town."

"There isn't any town up here." As I said it, the thought of a nearby community lifted my spirits. Maybe running away wouldn't be impossible if I knew which way to run.

"No, not up here. Be still."

Tool barked again. Closer now, as though she was headed back toward us. Then I heard something strange. Another bark. Yet it wasn't the same as the first. I'd read in a sporting magazine that dogs change voices as they pursue game. Maybe that explained the difference in her sounds.

My thumb touched the safety catch.

"Easy, boy."

"Okay."

"See that throat between the clumps?"

"Yes."

"Well, keep an eye on that open spot. The gap. Aim your piece at it. Lay down on your belly-gut and shoulder up."

I did what he told me.

"That's it," the old man whispered. "Now, release the safety so's you're at arm and ready."

Off to the right, I heard Tool running through the brush and wet leaves. Then I saw the blur of a dark dog kicking snow up in spurts with flying paws. Just a glimpse and then out of sight.

"Hold fast, boy."

"I'm holding."

"Be sure you don't—"

My eagerness failed to let Mr. Kirk finish his sentence. And if he did complete what he had to say, I never heard the rest of it.

I only saw the rabbit.

Out it came, just ahead of the dog, scampering over the mat of brown leaves and patches of snow. It stopped, uncertain about which way it would run. The bead of the barrel was right on its body as I squeezed the trigger, and the roar and recoil pounded into me.

As I saw the rabbit kick over, I yelled. "Got him!" The gun was shaking in my hands. And the gray afterburn of smoke didn't seem to bother me anymore. "I got him," I said once more.

Mr. Kirk let out a sigh.

Turning, I saw his face. His mouth was twisted into a dry scowl. But I didn't care. Handing him the gun, I raced down to the open area where the rabbit lay bloody and kicking. But before I could reach my kill, the dog came.

It wasn't Tool.

My mouth fell open. All I could do was stand there over the rabbit and look at the strange dog. He was coal black, darker than Tool, and nearly half again as large. A big dog that, at this moment, wore an ugly mouth. Lips curled back, he growled at me through his teeth.

I heard footsteps.

Then I saw a tall man coming up behind the dog. He leveled his shotgun at my chest, his finger rubbing the trigger. His face was covered with a bushy beard that was mostly black, with one streak of gray in it resembling a scar. On his head was a wide-brim floppy hat, also black. But what I mostly saw was the black hole of his gun.

The big man was breathing heavily. He said nothing. But his eyes shifted down to the rabbit and then back to me. Those eyes seemed to be the only two things that were alive in an otherwise dead face.

"Who be you?"

His voice was deep, unlike a human voice, more like the warning growl of some giant forest animal. He looked like a bear with clothes and a gun.

My mouth hung open, unable to speak.

Footsteps came. It was Mr. Kirk, moving about as fast as a man his age could. Tool was behind him. The black dog noticed Tool and growled, a ridge of hair stiffening along his spine. Tool held her own ground as her master spoke.

"It's my fault, Loomis. The boy's with me."

" 'Twas my dog."

"True. And it's your game."

I stepped closer to Mr. Kirk. "But I shot it. That rabbit's mine."

Scowling, the big man looked at Mr. Kirk and then spoke in his low voice. "Tell him."

"I will, Loomis."

The man called Loomis jerked up his gun and fired at the still rabbit, at close range, blowing blood and fur into nothing but wet dust. It was as though he had made the dead rabbit vanish. I felt hot urine gushing into my clothes.

I watched the smoke clear and the big man melt away into the brush. The black dog followed.

Tool snarled.

6

"Beans?"

The old man snorted. "That's all we got. But the living's worse where there ain't any."

"I'm not complaining. Just hungry."

"Then bow your head."

Mr. Kirk said his grace. "Lord, for this meal and for all Thy bounty, we tender our thanks. And we ask for no more but the forgiveness of our sins. Please bless our table and us in Thy serving. Amen."

"Amen," I said.

"Pity we don't got rabbit. Beans and a fry rabbit swallow real plentiful."

I put a fork of hot beans into my mouth. They tasted good. So I shoveled in two more bites before saying anything, watching the bean gravy melt down through my fork tines.

"That was our rabbit," I said. "Not *his*."

"Depends how you look to it."

"I shot it."

"Yup."

"Then by rights it ought to be on our table. Instead of wasted."

Mr. Kirk chewed and swallowed. "Collin, you don't never cut down game that's ahead of another man's dog."

"He didn't own that rabbit."

"But his dog did. What you done was take another man's food. By mountain manners, that amounts to thievery."

"Stealing?"

"You didn't intend to steal the meat. Intent is oft more meaningful than the act. But had I not been handy when you near put a hand on that rabbit . . ."

He didn't finish, but instead let his mouth take in more beans. I was grateful he hadn't gone on. Remembering the man made me shudder.

"Who is he?"

"His name is Loomis Broom."

Silently I repeated the name. Loomis Broom. It sent another chill down my backbone.

"He sure didn't act very friendly."

"Never does. All them Brooms want is to be left lonesome. They usual don't take what's mine, and I don't touch theirs. Until today. And it could breed sorrow, boy."

"Where do they live?"

"Nowhere, and all over. Back in the hills, mostly. A whole clan of Brooms north of here. And more to the west. Breed like summer flies."

"He was on your land."

"Nope, can't testify to that."

"How much land up here do you own?"

"None."

"Not any?"

"I'm what folks call a squatter."

"That word *squatter* is in history books."

"Oh?"

"Something to do with squatters' rights. I'm not really sure what I read about it. It wasn't too important."

"Squatters never be." The old man blew on his beans.

"Well, I guess I'm not very important either."

Mr. Kirk looked up through the bean steam. "Of course you are. Every person's important. And every tree and beast. Tool's important."

"At home, we have a dog. Her name's Winnie. She's a pedigreed poodle. What's Tool?"

"A dog. But she's mine and I'm hers."

"That dog of Loomis Broom's sure gave me the creeps. And so did old Loomis. He's a genuine spook."

"You're learning. So change the subject. I don't relish having a Broom for supper."

"These beans are really good."

"There's more in the pot on the stove. Go fetch yourself another helping."

In all the years I had lived at home, it was always my mother who jumped up from the table to refill our plates. Or to pour more coffee in Dad's cup. Standing at the big stove, I wondered if she knew where I was and if she was worrying. I sure didn't plan on staying here eating beans.

Mr. Kirk eyed my full plate. "You best swallow all that. Every blessed one. Hear?"

"I will."

"Maybe you'll add yourself a pound."

"Hope so. I'm kind of skinny."

"Same here. Only way to be. Lots of the down-hillers eat more than plenty."

My fork stopped. "Am I?"

"No. Heavens, eat away. I'm a growed man, but you're still stretching. Come fall, we'll butcher a pig and have pork in our beans all winter."

"You're going to get a pig?"

"Do every spring."

"How come you don't have a cow?"

"Don't need one. I don't drink milk, and I never did cotton to beef. Ain't a beefsteak in the world that can hold a candle to venison. A little spike or a forkhorn. Big old bucks is too tough on old teeth."

"I didn't understand what he was talking about, and I told him so. He explained. A spikehorn was a deer with two-pointed antlers. A forkhorn meant four points. "Venison is deer meat. And it beats beef. Keeps longer, too."

Looking around the interior of his small cabin, I didn't see a refrigerator. Or anything electrical.

"You don't have an icebox."

"No need."

"But all your stuff will spoil."

"Never has yet. Smells funny, but then I try it out on my taster."

"Your tongue?"

"No, on Tool. If'n the meat's turned, she won't touch it. Just turn up her nose and slink off. So I pitch it out to the coons. Often as not, you can cook the foul out of meat—if it's just ripe and not rotten. Believe me, I've et some real ripe rabbit. So ripe that the hair was falling."

I stopped eating.

"Don't fuss. Beans keep good."

"They do?"

"Yup. Anything dry keeps. If'n we smoke-dry venison, it'll weather all summer. Hang it and fang it, some say."

I cleaned the last bean off my white plate. Mr. Kirk watched me do it and almost smiled.

"Feel better?"

"Some."

"My old ma raised us on beans. Beans and belly."

"What's belly?"

"Underside pork. When times was good, we always baked pig in our beans. And when the lean times came, we ate beans alone. My mother could cook a pig's head like you couldn't believe."

I tasted every bean in my stomach. Trying to change the subject, I asked, "What do you feed Tool?"

"Scraps. She turned sour at us today."

"Why?"

"She knew we'd cut down a rabbit, so she was fixing to share in."

"Is that why she's sort of sulking outside the door?"

"Yup, that's why. Tool knew, when I was cooking, that there weren't no meat in that bean pot." Mr. Kirk held up both hands. "Don't ask how she knew. She just figures it. And right now, Tool is letting us both know what puny hunters we be, you and me."

"Aren't you going to feed her?"

"Nope. When she turns hungry enough, she'll wander off in the bush and fetch back a partridge. Spit out the feathers, chew the flesh raw, and even crack up the bone."

"Tool is quite a dog."

"She be. A real lady. I don't fret about her near half the way she worries over me."

"Is supper over?"

Mr. Kirk snorted. "Bet your belly button it's over. You choked in two plates of beans to my single. What in Sam Hill more do you want?"

"Dessert."

Sabbath Kirk scowled. "No chance."

7

"Wash or clean?"

"What do you mean?"

Mr. Kirk sighed. "Well, I meant do you preference to wash up the supper or clean the gun? You choose."

At the moment I didn't want to do either. All I wanted was to lie down on a long soft sofa and watch TV. But, as there was neither, I told Mr. Kirk that I'd tackle the dishes by myself and then help him clean the Purdey.

The dishes didn't take long. Two plates, a big spoon, two forks, and an empty bean pot. At least we had hot water, which I was told not to waste, from the big teakettle on the stove. And soap, which didn't do much to scour the bean pot until the old man added a handful of lake sand. He kept some in a bucket.

"Only two things'll scour a pot. Grit and gumption.

So git your elbow into it. Soap and sand'll do the remainder."

As I was scrubbing out the burned beans, I remembered our maid at home. She was someone I didn't think about very often because she was sort of like electricity. You just turned her on. Luroleen Bunkum was big and bustling and bossy. She told everybody in the whole house what to do—except for Winnie, our poodle, who hid whenever Luroleen came to clean.

Winnie hated the vacuum cleaner, and I hated Luroleen because all she ever said to me was one sentence. "Hogs wouldn't bed in your room, boy."

Luroleen had been with us for years and had scrubbed a pile of pots. It made me wish she'd walk into this cabin and take over. She'd probably even instruct poor old Mr. Kirk on how to clean his shotgun. Or grab the rag and do it herself.

Never did I dream the day would come when I'd miss Luroleen. I knew she wasn't missing me.

There was a scorched patch on the inside bottom of the pot that I attacked with soap, sand, and swearing. Even my thumbnail. Speck by speck, it scrubbed loose. The old man limped over to inspect my work. I held up the pot.

"Is it clean enough?"

"Too clean. I don't believe a cook ought to pamper a pot. It'll do."

The daylight was fading. To the west, I could no longer see pink beneath the tops of the pines. I was sort of glad for the window over the sink, even if the sink didn't have any faucets. If a mountain could have a slum, this was it.

Mr. Kirk lit a candle on the table. Nights were going to be long in Vermont, I was thinking.

He showed me how to disassemble the Purdey, clean it, oil it, and put all the parts back together. It was a single-shot gun. Not very intricate. So I mastered the job in not much more time than it had taken to scrub the bean pot. I snapped the gun shut.

"There," I said. "That was easy."

Kirk wrinkled his nose. "Fair."

"Now what?"

"Let's step outdoors. I welcome April on account the bugs aren't out yet. Too frosty."

We went outside.

"Hey, it's cold out here."

"It'll get colder come dark," he said.

"Spring's coming."

"Maybe to down south. You're in north country, and' April can wheel shifty."

I was grateful to be wearing a heavy wool sweater. In addition, I buttoned the collar button of my blue Oxford-cloth shirt.

"If the stove's in there," I said, "it doesn't make a whole lot of sense to be out here."

"What are you, boy? Some delicate breed of hothouse plant?"

"No. Just so cold my teeth are chattering."

"Well, go inside if you're of a mind to. And miss all the doing."

Not wanting to miss whatever he was talking about, I asked him what the big deal was. He didn't answer, but circled his arm for me to follow. So I did.

We climbed up on a high rock west of the cabin. It wasn't really high, but about thirty or forty feet above the roof. The old man puffed a bit, but his wishbone legs made the climb.

"See it?"

"No."

"Right over yonder."

Looking where Sabbath Kirk was pointing, I saw the last ember of sunset sink into a V-notch formed by two distant peaks.

"Are those the Green Mountains?"

"That they be. Leastwise, they were this morning. As a fact, we've got the Green Mountains pretty much all around us."

"Do you look at that view every evening?"

"Nope, 'cause it don't happen every night. Only for a few weeks in April and again come August. Sun has to set just so. Real pretty, eh?"

I admitted it was. Never before had I seen so vibrant a sky in so confined an area. It was a tiny flaming triangle that rested on a long and dark and jagged mountain silhouette that resembled a sleeping man.

"Somebody," I said, "ought to give that chunk of sunset a name."

"Already have."

"You named it?"

"Yup."

"Well, what's it called?"

"I call it War Head."

Looking at War Head again, still afire, I decided that few poets could have blessed it with a better name. For that was what it appeared to be—a flaming arrowhead about to plunge into a giant sleeping warrior of a mountain range.

"Seeing it makes me almost hear things," I told the old man.

"Such as?"

"Oh, the death scream of a Mohawk warrior, or maybe a Huron. It's a sad, burning death. Maybe even a song. Some maiden weeping for her fallen brave." As I described what I pictured, I felt as if I'd said way too much about a distant miracle that needed no description at all.

"That's what I've thought, too," said the old man. "Guess I never quite put it all into words as well as you done."

"Dad calls me a ham."

"No, you're not. After the supper you packed away, I'd guess you're a bean."

"The color's fading. I can see the giant warrior dying, growing cold and still, sleeping in darkness. Gosh, I wish I were an Indian. Seeing outdoor stuff like this always makes me—corny."

Mr. Kirk squinted at me. "Corny?"

"You know. Like I feel there's a religion up in the sky that my hand can't reach out and touch. Yet I know it's there."

"How do you know certain?"

"I just saw it. Honest. If I ever start up a new religion, it'll have something to do with the War Head."

"Oh, really?"

"Yeah, really. What I mean is, how could any dumb kid like me ever look at a sight like that and be an atheist?"

"Or an old kid like me?"

"You feel it, too, I guess."

Mr. Kirk nodded. "Every time."

"Can you see it during the day?"

"Only the notch. Just a sawtooth on the horizon that don't capture much notice. Unless you know where to look. Even so, it ain't a sight. The War Head begs evening."

"It's still dying."

"It be."

"I wonder if we climbed up higher, up on some of these crags, if we could see it longer."

"Nope. I tried it once."

"You saw nothing?"

"Saw the sunset. But I couldn't see the War Head. It was like I'd imagined the whole shebang. The arrowhead was clean gone."

"I'd like to have my mother see it sometime. Just the way we saw it tonight."

"Your ma's a pretty lady."

"How do you know?"

"Because your pa showed me her picture."

"Yeah, she is sort of beautiful, now that you mention it. There's something kind of holy about her face."

"Makes me wonder."

"About what?"

"How she dropped an ugly colt like you."

8

Sabbath Kirk shivered.

"Gotcha," I said. "You're as cold out here as I am. But I don't feel like going inside just yet."

"Neither do I. You know, I been cooped up in that shack since Christmas, and the outdoors feels good. It's a fresh cold."

"We could use our coats."

"S'pose so." Mr. Kirk climbed down from the last rock step.

"I'll get them."

Running inside, I fished my coat out of my suitcase. It was a red-and-black buffalo plaid that I'd gotten from Dad on my last birthday. All wool. Next to my new one, Mr. Kirk's old gray jacket looked worn and shoddy. It made me wonder how the old geezer was going to afford to pay me even a dollar a month.

"Here's yours." I tossed him his coat.

"Thanks."

"Well, now that I've seen the War Head, what else is there around here to see at night?"

"Depends."

Hands on my hips, I waited with all my patience for him to say more. I wanted to yell, "Depends on what?" at him. Darn him and his half ideas. Finally I couldn't wait him out.

"On what?" I asked.

"Oh, guess it sometimes leans on whether Tool's stayed or gone."

Looking around, I didn't see her. "Tool?"

"No use to call her. She won't come to you."

"Where is she?"

"Run off," said the old man.

"Maybe she'll bring home a partridge." As I said it, I knew I was faking, because it was a mystery to me just what a partridge was. Some bird.

As if Sabbath Kirk could read my mind, he just stood there, squinting at me, and then said, "Some folks call it a ruffed grouse." He held his hands about a foot apart. "It's this long, brown, with a fan tail."

"Yeah," I said. "I know."

"You'll certain know if you ever startle one out of the brush. Takes off and roars like a mad bull."

I felt the wool collar of my coat scratching my neck, beneath my chin. It was a cozy feeling. My mind was trying not to think about home.

"If we're in luck tonight, Bandit'll come."

"Who's he?" I was hoping that Bandit, whoever he

would be, was no relation to Loomis Broom. Or his dog.

"Reckon you'll see for yourself." The old man looked to the north of the cabin. "Seeing as Tool's not around to interfere. Best we sit and hush up. He'll come."

Mr. Kirk was right. Bandit came.

The two of us were sitting on a slab bench that rested against the north exposure of the shack, leaning ourselves back, our spines on the cross logs. Just waiting in the dark silence. When I was getting bored with it all, Mr. Kirk reached over very slowly to touch the sleeve of my jacket.

I looked where he was looking, wanting to whisper, "Is that Bandit?" But I kept mum.

Along he came. As the old man had predicted, he came from the direction of the pond that I'd seen earlier, north of the cabin. Two black eyes were shining at us, seeing us as we both watched him.

"Come, Bandit." The old man's voice was soft and easy. "I got a boy here who never seed a raccoon, so prance along."

Bandit was a good name for the little animal. Across his eyes was a strip of dark fur, blacker than the night was becoming, that resembled a tiny mask.

"Is he tame?"

"Not so's you'd notice. Hush now, boy, and let him whiff the pair of us, or he'll shy off and skedaddle."

The moon burst from behind a cloud, and I could

see Bandit coming closer to us. Hesitating with each step of his paws.

"Now then, Bandit, we got a visitor here for you to meet up with. A city boy who wants to greet you proper. But he'll keep his hands to home because he knows how sharp your teeth be. If he don't, he'll learn right quick."

Bandit stopped, less than twenty feet away.

"He's smelling around for Tool. Don't ask me how he knows she's run off, but he figures it. Don't you, Bandit?"

The old man began to hum. My ear couldn't decipher any particular melody, only his own tune of timeless music that a tone-deaf grandfather might hum to a sleepy child.

"I don't guess I remember too many songs," Mr. Kirk whispered. "But old Bandit ain't too particular on how sorry I warble."

The raccoon's body was full and furry, the hair on his paws and legs glistening, wet with pond water. His feet must have felt really cold, because earlier today I had noticed that the lake was still partly frozen. The water, when I had bent to drink, was liquid ice. So cold it made my throat ache.

"Do you feed him?"

In answer, the old man pulled a peanut shell from his pocket. "One peanut is all I afford him. Otherwise, he'd forfeit his freedom. And I don't relish that."

"Will he come and take it?"

"Show him, Bandit. Come along and taste your treat."

Bandit edged closer. Seeing the peanut, the coon sat up on his hind legs, his black nose stretching forward toward us as far as his neck would allow.

"Boy, lock your hands in your pockets and don't even twitch an itch. Hear?"

"I hear."

"A wild coon ain't no household pet, and he's got fangs that'll rip open a dog. You reach out a hand to stroke him and folks'll maybe call you Lefty."

I almost laughed. And I wondered why the old man never smiled whenever he'd crack a joke. It made me think about all the stand-up comics I'd seen on TV. Always laughing but rarely funny. I was suddenly aware of my countless hours on the sofa, watching TV sitcoms and never laughing.

Bandit charged, grabbed the peanut with his front paws, and hurried away.

"Let's hit the feathers, boy. Morning wakes up early."

"I'm not sleepy. What time is it?"

"Bedtime."

"Don't you have a watch? I didn't even spot a clock in the cabin."

"Had a watch once. Gave it away. Dang thing kept stopping 'cause I'd not recall to crank her up. A fool can tell twixt day and dark."

In the cabin, I asked him where I was to sleep. There was only one narrow cot.

"On the floor."

"It'll be too hard."

"I forgot."

He went outside while I skinned off my clothes and unfolded a clean pair of flannel pajamas that Mom had insisted I take along. They felt good to climb into, warm and welcoming.

Mr. Kirk returned with a dripping armful of needles and pine boughs, which he dumped with little ceremony beneath the table on the far side of the cabin.

"Here."

"On *that?*"

"You'll get accustomed. May take some habituating, but I done it more 'n once. Besides, it smells sweet."

I hated it. It was worse than sleeping on a bag of doorknobs, especially when I saw the old man, in his long gray underwear, snuff out the candle, and then heard him creaking into his cot, singing the rusty springs.

The old duffer hadn't so much as grunted a goodnight. But who cared? I felt angry with myself. For sure, I had no intention of becoming his friend or his damn hired hand. He wasn't going to buy *me* the way he was trying to buy a raccoon, with a peanut. No way. Yet I'd have to watch my step with Tool and never blow my cool and punch the old guy.

Damn it! Why had I reversed my feelings and gone soft, tagging along with every suggestion Kirk made? I should have kept my distance and kept quiet, giving the old man little more than silence. He sure was a talkative old codger. And I was a jerk to listen and look at the War Head the way I did.

But I couldn't help it. It was like seeing an evening prayer. Stuff like that always got to me, and I wasn't ashamed of it. But I wished I hadn't talked about it. No matter how it seemed, Kirk was still a watchdog over me, and this was a prison, and I was a prisoner.

Dad had lied. Listening to the old man breathe, I thought about how to get away. My so-called pay was a joke. At a dollar a month, it would take forever to buy so much as a bus ticket home. I began to wonder where Kirk hid his money. In a cabin this size, there couldn't be too many nooks to search.

I'd just wait my chance.

9

I rolled over. Beneath me, the pine boughs rustled, as if to warn me that I wasn't going to go to sleep very soon. Not much like my comfortable bed back in Greenwich.

Well, here I am, I thought with a sigh. But that doesn't mean I have to stay. There aren't any fences. Just miles of frozen geography in each and every direction. I know which way north is, though. It's up toward the lake.

When I skip, I'll head due south. Down to the road and back toward Middlebury or to some of those other little towns. Maybe find a job. Doing what? Probably washing dishes in some greasy-spoon diner or pumping gas at a filling station. The pay wouldn't be great.

But it'd sure beat three cents a day! I snorted. Kirk had to be kidding. Nobody in his right mind would work all day for three lousy pennies. Nobody except me. Of course, I'd be hard pressed to dig up three people who'd testify that Collin Richardson Pepper *was* in his right mind.

I thought back on all my trips to see Dr. Rutledge. At least I didn't have to lie down on some stupid sofa and make up stories about how much I hated my mother. Just had to sit in that rocking chair and tell Rutledge whatever came to mind. Nothing ever did. So I made it all up.

It was like a game. Every lie I could think of, I told Dr. Rutledge. Not a grain of truth in any of it. Especially about how I'd always wanted to murder someone, just to see if I could pull it off and get away with it.

"Easy," I'd told him. "I could ice my math teacher, Mr. Wall at Greenwich High, and then plead insanity. After all, Doc, I'm seeing an analyst. Here I am in your handsome oak-paneled office. So I must be bonkers. Out of my gourd."

What jury would convict a crazy kid?

I told Dr. Rutledge fib upon fib. How I was planning to waste everybody in town as soon as I bought my machine gun. Mow 'em all down.

"Why?" he'd asked.

"Because I hate everybody. That's why."

Trouble is, I really don't hate anyone at all. No, that's wrong. Sometimes I hate Collin Pepper. And I have more than a hunch I'm not going to grow too fond of Mr. Kirk over there. Or his dog.

How about Loomis Broom? Now *there's* a hate object.

Funny, but Mr. Kirk doesn't seem to hate Loomis. Maybe the old man's like me. Doesn't hate anybody. Inside, he might even like people. He likes Dad.

I don't. And my father must not care a whole lot for me, or else he wouldn't have stuck me up here in this stinkpot of a shack, with a mean old man and a dog that's even meaner.

"Tool." I whispered her name to the darkness.

If I ran away, would Mr. Kirk order Tool to chase after me and track me through the woods? And then, when I was breathless and falling down, Tool would overtake me and finish me off—the way hounds finally rip apart a fox.

I remembered a movie I'd seen late at night on television. Some poor slob in wet rags was running through a swamp. Not too quickly because of leg irons and a chain. He'd escaped from some prison. Devils Island? Anyhow, the bloodhounds were after him. Only they weren't bloodhounds. They were Dobermans.

Behind the dogs came men with guns. I was hoping that the criminal, whoever he was, would finally get away. But he didn't. He made a good try, running as best he could, sloshing through the mist and the swamp water. Probably lost. Crazy? No, just confused.

"You're a confused boy, Collin." That's what Dr. Rutledge told me. Psychiatrists never level with a kid and tell him that he's just plain nuts. Not when his parents are forking over thirty-five bucks per session.

Confused is the word they use. How come they don't say *twisted* or *warped* or a *mite touched in the head?*

So run, Collin. Splash through the swamp and you'll escape from Devils Island—and the old head devil snoring a few feet away on his cot.

Where will I go, though?

Grandfather would take me in. He's getting a bit long of tooth, and his hearing isn't first class, but he's a lot more than just a grandfather. More like an old pal. He's my best friend.

I guess, in his day, he was one heck of a super surgeon. Grandfather is the only person in the world I would dare tell that I might want to be a doctor someday. The rest of my family would laugh in my face. But he'd believe me. Because he'd know that any secret I told him would be true. Straight from my heart.

He never comes right out and says he wants me to be a doctor. But he does.

There's a big red leather chair in his study, and back when I was little, I used to sit there in his lap, and together we'd examine the pictures in his medical books. We'd flip through the books, skipping all the print, until we'd come to a photograph. In color. Then he'd tell me what all the glands were and how each functioned, within what he always called "the marvelous machine of man."

So I grew up asking him to tell me a "body story" rather than a fairy tale. Sometimes he told me about the heart. It was just a very tough muscle. Tough, because it worked all the time as a pump. The lungs were pumps too. Our blood was a supply line, and the stomach was a food-processing plant. Guts were sewers, drainpipes.

"Whenever the body machine breaks down," he'd said, "that's when a doctor rolls up his sleeves and goes to work making repairs. Like a mechanic under a car."

It made sense.

"How many machines can you fix?" I'd asked him.

Seeing that his hair was so white, and he always worked such long hours at the hospital, I guess I already knew the answer. Lots of machines. I wasn't very old when I asked him one particular question. "Why didn't you fix up Grandmother?"

She had died some months earlier. And when I asked him, he had to take off his glasses and not look at me for a while. I knew he missed her as much as I did. So, instead of pressing him for an answer, I put my arms around his neck and hugged him hard.

I wanted to hug Grandfather right now.

He sure was a different kind of man than Mr. Kirk. But possibly the same age. Their voices weren't much alike. Grandfather usually talked as though he were reading something important out of a book or reciting a famous poem. Mr. Kirk talked as if he'd never read a book at all. Yet I sort of liked the way he said things.

Rolling over onto my side, I felt the floor's hardness hammer my hip.

My parents could never understand why I didn't jump out of bed in the morning and whistle into a fresh day. I tried to tell Mom and Dad that usually I'd been awake for most of the night.

"Doing what?" Dad would ask.

"Nothing. I just think about stuff."

Father would snort and then remark that I never gave much thought to my schoolwork, because my grades were never too great.

Well, dear Father, I thought, up here in the Vermont wilderness, there aren't going to be any report cards. Or am I wrong? Is this ordeal just one more test for me to flunk? One more hurdle to trip over?

Of course, nobody could blame my parents for not being too proud of me. I wasn't a pro at anything. My piano lessons were a dismal failure. I didn't like to practice all those boring exercises that were about as melodic as our door buzzer.

"Music isn't a buzzer, Mom," I told her. "It's chimes."

So instead of reading notes on a sheet of music, I liked to sit at our piano when no one else was home and pick out tunes with one finger. Any time I did it, Winnie would saunter over, lie down under the piano, and rest her chin on my foot. Sometimes her tail would wag.

But then, a few days later, I'd usually take a lot of

grief from Miss Golder, my piano teacher, because I hadn't practiced any of her dumb exercises. During one lesson in particular, I sort of went crazy and asked Miss Golder to lie down under the piano and rest her chin on my foot, so I could play her a melody that I'd composed and see if she'd wag her tail.

She blew up. That was the day she telephoned Mother to announce that my piano lessons were to be suspended and that I was a "very *disturbed* boy."

This was the chief incident that prompted my early visits to Dr. Rutledge. Unlike piano lessons, these sessions were twice a week instead of only once. And there wasn't any music. Just a stream of door-buzzer conversation, mostly from me, that buzzed out of my mouth and into his little secret notebook.

I talked sentences. He punctuated, grunting out an "I see" or an occasional "Oh?"

Dr. Rutledge pretended to listen. I always had the feeling that he wished *he* were lying on a couch taking a nap. He did listen, I suppose. Yet he never heard. Not even when I was screaming. I wasn't hollering out loud, but from inside—as the bloodhounds were chasing me through a misty swamp. And I didn't know which way to run because I was alone and cold.

Devils Island, you see, is a frightening place in Greenwich, Connecticut, that nobody knows about.

Except me.

10

"Get up, boy."

It was dark and cold in the cabin. Trying to roll over, I realized how stiff my body had become during the night.

"What time is it?"

"Morning."

Mr. Kirk certainly stockpiled a bunch of sparkling answers. Right then, I hated him and hated his floor, pine boughs and all. To make my night even less comfortable, I had also dreamed of Loomis Broom.

"Why are we getting up so stinking early?"

Sabbath Kirk snorted. "Work."

The word made me wince. And wonder what kind of chores the old man did up here. There wasn't any office to go to, or a factory. Rubbing my eyes, I sat up on my bedroll and saw that Mr. Kirk was already dressed. Then I heard Tool outside the door.

"Your dog's back."

"No surprise."

Stripping off my flannel pajamas, I put on yesterday's clothes. My socks smelled dirty, but I didn't much care, because my feet were even dirtier. Mr. Kirk looked at me.

"Go wash."

"Where?"

"Outside. You'll spy it. If the bucket's empty, go fill 'er up."

"All the way to the lake?"

"Nope. If you recall the rocks we stood on, watching the War Head, you'll find a freshet around to the right, past a stand of deer fern."

A freshet? Well, whatever it was, maybe the bucket wouldn't be empty, and I wouldn't have to ask what I was told to search out. I opened the door and saw Tool, who darted by me and into the shack. The bucket was half water and half ice. A slightly soiled towel hung on a peg and served to dry my face and hands. Then I splashed some water on my freezing feet.

To the east, I saw a sliver of sun peeking through the pines. Back inside, I asked Mr. Kirk what we were having for breakfast, fully intending to return to bed if he answered beans. Last night's supper had turned me into a gas pump.

"Corn bread."

As he spoke, I smelled the stove. It had been poked alive while I was outside and was giving off a muffin smell.

"Is there any orange juice?"

"Nope. But there's coffee. Look over yonder in that big can. No, the sugar's in that one. To the far side of the shelf. Search instead of ask and you'll find it quicker."

"Found it."

"You brew the coffee. I'm busy with my baking."

"I don't know how."

"Then learn or stay thirsty."

I boiled some water in the teakettle, poured it into two white mugs, and let a heaping spoon of grainy coffee fall twice into the mugs. Then I stirred it, hoping it would muddy into something that was fit to drink. The old man took one burning sip and made a face.

"You ain't much of a cook."

"How do *you* make it?"

"Same way. And it tastes just as sorry."

"Then I guess you're not much of a cook either."

"Never claimed I was."

I had made up my mind not to like his corn bread. Yet when he took a bent knife, cut a healthy yellow square, and placed it steaming on my white plate, it smelled like heaven. Before I could break off a corner, he barked at me.

"Hold it."

"Why?"

"It ain't done."

Pulling a dusty cork out of a small gray jar, Mr. Kirk doused my corn bread with a torrent of sauce.

"What's that? Syrup?"

"Honey."

I ate it all and asked for more, which he tossed on my sticky plate. Like last evening's beans, the breakfast wasn't very fancy, but it was filling. The coffee tasted better with each gulp.

"What'll we have for lunch?"

"Nothing. Tool and me eat twice a day, and it seems to serve our souls in full measure. We eat breakfast and supper. Noontime's for working."

Swell, I thought. Not even light yet, and the old cuss is planning to take his three cents out of my hide, with no lunch. The old skinflint. Maybe I could report him to the Vermont authorities so he'd be indicted for breaking the child labor law. Then I remembered that I'd eaten three meals here and not done any real work.

"I'll wash up the breakfast," I said.

Mr. Kirk raised his eyebrows. "Sure it won't be too much of a strain? Hate to witness you falling over in a dead faint from labor."

In the baking pan, one corner of corn bread remained. I ate half of it, and the other part went to Tool as soon as the old man moistened it with a finger of bacon grease. The dog seemed to be starving as she snapped it all up with one bite. No wonder Tool was so skinny.

"Let's be starting." Mr. Kirk moved toward the door.

"Do we bring our jackets?"

"Nope. Work'll warm us righteous sudden." He

pulled down an ax, and we went outdoors where he pointed at a shrunken woodpile. Lots of bark lay on the hard, bare ground. "There," he said. "That's where it'll go. And I don't favor it throwed there. I want my wood piled neater than a preacher's whistle."

I sighed. "Okay."

Northeast of the shack, we came to his source of firewood—plenty of fallen trees. I knew the difference between green wood and dry, having heard Dad swear at our fireplace every Christmas and having watched him cough in the smoke because he'd also forgotten to open the damper.

Dad and machinery, any sort, were bitter enemies.

"Boy, this here's an ax."

"I know. Don't you ever imagine I know *anything?*"

"Yup, you do. Enough to whack your foot in twain, or let the head skip up and lop off your kneecap. An ax is a tricky customer. Mean as sin. Axes seem to guess when a man is alone in the woods before they kick up ornery."

"Okay, okay."

"Just so's you understand that it be a tool and not a toy."

"Which tree do you want me to chop down?"

"None. All I want you to do is learn what an ax can do to a man's person as well as his pine."

Boy, I thought, he sure can be one tiresome teacher. It doesn't take any brains to figure out an ax. Or to use one. I'll show him.

"I'm ready."

"Very well. Try 'er out."

The ax was double-bitted, with a wing of sharp silver on both ends of the blade. He handed it to me, and I was surprised to find it weighed about twice what I had imagined.

"Here goes."

With a bit of theatrics, I spat on both hands, then hacked away at a fallen trunk that was about telephone-pole size. Gripping the handle in clenched fingers, I beat the wood straight down, giving the log more than twenty blows—and cutting only the bark.

"Slant it," Kirk said.

"What?"

"Angle your stroke, one side and then the other, so's a wedge of the wood'll pop free."

"I know. I'm just warming up."

Trying it his way made all the difference. Hunks of dead pine split off as I chopped lower and lower into the dark heart.

I stopped for breath. "It gets tougher down near the bottom."

"Roll 'er over."

In the clover, I thought. Should I share the joke? Best not. Vermonters weren't very fond of humor, I'd been told. "Roll the ax over?"

"No, the log. You won't have to cut so deep or bend so lowly. And, if'n there be a nested rock under the timber, you don't bust your blade into the cusser."

"Sure." I kicked the log over and pulled off my sweater, not bothering to recomb my hair. Rolling up the sleeves of my blue shirt, I lifted the ax once again, keeping my hands tightly together on the long handle.

"Choke your right hand, lad."

"What for?"

"It'll ply your ax easier if'n you slide your right hand up toward the head on your upswing. Then let 'er slide back, hands united, on your cut stroke. Try it."

I refused. Instead, I just hacked away, becoming so winded that I was woozy. Finally, I cut through.

"Your turn." I handed him the ax with shaking arms and watched him work. His swing was smooth, almost effortless, and the chips flew faster than flushed birds. To cut through that same log, I had used close to a hundred blows. So I counted his.

Sabbath Kirk did it in twenty-eight.

11

We cut through the morning.

When I used the ax, the old man lugged the cut wood back to his cabin. And as he chopped and split, I toted load after load. The work made me wet with sweat.

Mr. Kirk noticed my perspiration. "That's the way it be with firewood."

I smirked back at him. "The way *what* be?"

"Warms you before you even burn it."

"Are we going to work this hard all day?"

"Only to sundown."

I sighed. "I hate it."

"So do I."

"You do?"

"Yup."

"Then why are you grinning at me?"

Mr. Kirk wrinkled his smile a bit deeper. "Because I like to watch you work. You're soft. But days like today'll belt your belly."

"Swell."

"Hop to it. Load yourself up and burden them kindling to the cabin. You piling it neat like I told you?"

"Yes. I even straightened what was already there that you'd messed up."

"Good. When you return from your next trip, fetch back that long pull-saw that you'll find hanging by the pile. Under the eave."

"Which one? There're two there."

"It's got a handle to each end. You'll see it, unless you're blinder than a fool in love."

I brought the saw, taking my time about it, so I wouldn't have to break my back, which was already starting to ache.

"Do you want me to saw this log?" I asked.

"We'll both cut 'er, in concert."

"Suits me."

"It's a two-man saw, so she'll take two men to make 'er sing."

"Sorry. All we have," I told him, "is a man and a boy."

Sabbath Kirk squinted at me. "A boy who works hard as a man and leans into a man's work sprouts up quick."

With a fallen tree between us, we rested the teeth of the long saw across the trunk. Before starting, I loosened my shirt, knowing that I wasn't going to get any cooler. Not in *his* company.

He pulled his saw handle with both hands as I hung on to the handle at my end. So then I pulled, too. And pushed. But the saw bucked, bending the blade and causing the old man to scowl at me.

"I pull; then you pull. Ain't no push to it. Just turns, you and then me. Got it?"

I nodded. The old know-it-all thought he knew everything. Maybe he did, about *saws*.

"Pull."

I pulled, then waited as he yanked the saw back into his shirt. The saw chewed into the dry wood. Next to my knee on the ground, the dead leaves began to be frosted with specks of sawdust. Watching his hands, I marked how his fingers relaxed on the handle as I took my turn. He rested between each of his pulls. So I did "the likewise," as he phrased it.

Deeper and deeper, the teeth tore into the cut until we were halfway through. He stopped pulling to wipe his face with a gray sleeve.

"Do we roll the log over now?"

"Yup."

We made our second cut, and I finally noticed the freed section loosen. It was only about a foot long, so when split, the kindling would fit under a pair of the black griddles of the big Acme American stove.

We stopped. Looking up through the tall pines, I saw the April sun at an angle, tinted green as the sunbeams filtered down through the needles and cones.

"I wonder what time it is," I said.

"You going somewhere?"

"Eventually."

"Don't let me tarry you, boy. If'n you got yourself a mind to leave, I won't stop you. So long."

"You *want* me to go, don't you?"

"Go or work."

I snorted. "At a dollar a month? Three cents a day?"

"That's right. Dollar plus your keep. No extra charge for my good cookery or that comfy bed you slept on last night."

I groaned. Sabbath Kirk was probably getting his jollies over the fact that he slept on a cot while the floor was all mine.

"Now, if things simmer out between us—I'm not promising they will—yet if'n they do, maybe we'll build you a bunk."

"With a rock mattress, I suppose."

Sabbath Kirk smiled. "Nope. We can fix you up decent."

"I bet." As I spoke, I spat out a sawdust speck.

"Collin, I'm a Vermonter."

"What does that mean? Okay, so you're a Vermonter. Is that supposed to be something special?"

"It means that when I tell you something, be it sweet or sorry, I mean every word. You and me ain't to tell each other stories. Whatever you say to me, I'll listen it as straight out and not ponder a word of it. I figure that if you be your pa's whelp, then you'll prosper up to be a down-the-middle man. Enough talk. So we'll have at it. Both shoulder our share."

"That's fair."

"Good. Let's work."

We worked. I tugged my end of the saw after each yank of his, pulling until I thought my arms were going to be jerked off my shoulders. My hands hurt. Yet I swore I'd not gripe about it. If I couldn't out-work a tired old man, then I wasn't much of a kid.

Watching the face of Sabbath Kirk as I pulled the saw, I waited for a sign that he was getting as tired as I was. Saying nothing, he continued to pull the saw through cut after cut, pausing only to kick over the log or bite the teeth into a fresh mark. Finally I just had to stop for a breath.

"Are we ever going to quit?"

"We'll quit, yes."

"When?"

"Soon's we get the job settled. That's the time to quit. Not before. A man don't measure drowsy. He measures *done*."

My hands were hurting more with every move of the long saw. They hurt so badly that I felt as though a scream was about to come out of my mouth. I wanted to swear at him, because he didn't seem to care about how tired we both were becoming. His face had started to twitch as he pulled, and I noticed that the saw's grinding noise was not as loud as it had been earlier.

Perhaps I was going deaf. Or dumb.

Closing my eyes as I worked the saw, I tried think-ing about other things. About me. Collin Richardson

Pepper, lumberjack. I made an effort not to say silently Collin Richardson Pepper, candy-ass. I wanted Josh Witten to see me now. At least there wasn't any clean white paper lining the bottoms of my drawers. I didn't even have a drawer. My stuff was still salted away in my two suitcases, collecting wrinkles.

I tried prayer, trying to think of the War Head.

"Enough."

Looking up, I saw Sabbath Kirk pull a red bandana out of his pocket and wipe his forehead. Now was my chance to put him down.

"It's not sundown yet," I said. "And the job isn't done. Don't tell me you have to quit and go take your afternoon nap."

"You got a mean mouth, boy."

"Oh, really?"

"Had a mule once, and she had a mean mouth. So I had to shoot 'er and eat 'er. But it turned out she was even too tough to chew."

"I don't believe it."

"Neither do I, 'cause I'm just fibbing you."

"Vermonters don't fib."

"Some do, and some don't. Right now, when I look you in the eye and tell you my back's near broke on this tomfool saw, it ain't no story. How do you feel, boy?"

I didn't want to lie to him. "Pooped. When I said let's do more sawing, I was telling you a story. My arms are about to drop off. Are we finished?"

"Near to."

"How much more?"

"One cut. Then we'll burden what we split and pile her to home."

I let out a deep breath. "Thank God."

Pulling an apple out of his pocket, Mr. Kirk tossed it over the log to my hand. Then he bit into an apple of his own. My mouth took a loud and generous bite.

"How's she taste?"

"Good," I said. "Thanks."

"You're welcome. These two is the last pair out of the barrel. No more until near October."

We ate beans for supper.

It was all my arm could do to lift up my fork with only three or four beans on it. Five would have ruptured my muscles. Hip to hip at the sink, we washed the supper dishes together, saying little.

The old man yawned. So did Tool, even though she had slept almost all day.

I went outside the cabin to empty my bladder on the rough trunk of a pine. By the time I returned, Mr. Kirk was in his underwear, on his cot, under his blankets. As I fell down on my bedroll, the boughs and needles didn't feel so hard. My whole body had stiffened to stone. I wanted the old man to tell me that today I'd earned my corn bread and plate of beans. All he did was snore.

In the dark, I smiled to myself. For the first time in my life, I'd done a day's work. Luroleen, I thought, you'd be proud.

12

My body ached. Yet my mind didn't seem to hurt—
an odd feeling, one I had never experienced before.
My bed was far from soft, but it felt softer than the
night before because my arms and legs seemed to be
harder.

I envied Mr. Kirk and his remarkable ability to drift
off into snoring in less than a minute after he'd
crashed on his cot.

Man, we'd sure split and stacked a supply of wood
today. How long would it take to burn it all up in the
big black Acme American? I couldn't take another
day like today. No, that was wrong. I could. I could
take any pesky chore that the old man got the notion
to dish out.

Three cents for all that work! I couldn't believe I'd
done it. Well, I'm three pennies richer than I was this
morning, I thought. It almost made me laugh.

Earlier, when the two of us were washing up before
supper, I had asked Mr. Kirk how he earned his liv-

ing. He'd told me he was a guide. That much I already knew. But there didn't seem to be many hunters around. Loomis Broom surely wasn't one of Mr. Kirk's clients.

I shuddered. The thought of old Loomis chilled my spine.

"Howdy there, Loomis," I whispered to myself in the dark. "My name's Collin Pepper. I'm from Greenwich, Connecticut, and my father works on Wall Street. Impressed? Well now, Loomis old chap, there's going to be a few changes made around here. Not that I intend to sound uppity, but I've been giving a bit of thought to that charming custom of yours. You know, the rule that claims I can't gun a rabbit when it's a step or two ahead of your dog."

Closing my eyes, I could picture Broom's black animal. Never had I seen a dog like that. A mouth that curled into a machine of teeth. A real chopper.

That dog sure wasn't Winnie.

My half-asleep mind saw two dogs in a fighting pit. One was Winnie; the other was Loomis's black dog. His dog was snarling at Winnie, making her cringe. Poor old Winnie, who was afraid of the noise the vacuum cleaner made whenever Luroleen jockeyed it from room to room.

I wondered if Loomis had ever seen a vacuum cleaner.

As the black dog sprang at Winnie's throat, the horrible image forced my eyes to open, to make the dogfight dissolve into the blank void of a cabin wall.

I've got to sleep, I told myself. And then I wondered, smiling, is this what people mean when they talk about being *dog tired?* You're still awake, eyes open, yet you're half-dreaming of dogs and hearing them snarl.

Tool and Broom's dog sure are hunters. I wonder when some human hunters will come and hire Mr. Kirk as their guide? Do city people hunt up here in April? Probably not often. The old man said his work was seasonal. Hunters in the fall and fishermen in spring. Not much guide business this time of year, according to Mr. Kirk.

I wonder where he buys his food. At the rate I'm forking in the beans, we'll need to take a trip to the store before too long. Maybe the old duck will give me some money and send me to haul back supplies. If he does, he'll never see *me* again. The guy owes me a lot more than three cents for today's labor.

Still, I'm not crazy about the idea of stealing his chow money. To split this crummy scene is one thing, but to pocket his grubstake, or whatever he calls it, is something else.

I thought of the rabbit. My ears still heard the report of Loomis Broom's big shotgun, and once again the rabbit exploded into a spatter of blood and fur dust. Nobody would ever steal *his* bread.

It was a chilling thought to consider what Broom would have done to me if Mr. Kirk had not come panting up to intervene on my behalf. The old man showed no fear of Broom, not one blink of an eye or hesitant word. Kirk was no coward. I was scared skinny, but *he* wasn't. There just wasn't any flinch in Sabbath Kirk.

"No," I whispered to the wall, "I'll never steal his money. Even if it means I can't run away without it. I'm no thief."

But would he trust me? Would the old man actually hand me a few bucks and send me on a grocery errand? Well, if he did, he was in for one hell of a shocker. I'd return with his stupid stores.

Just like the old buzzard to test me.

But if you do, old man, you won't be able to report to Dad that you bought out his kid for a few lousy dollars. Am I weakening? Up that. It's not weakness to be honest. Dad says that criminals are the weaklings, and I figure it adds up.

Anyhow, after seeing how little Mr. Kirk has, and how hard he works to lug his firewood, I'd be a real squirrel to split and rip him off.

"Pepper," I said, "not even you."

Several of the kids I knew in Greenwich were pulling off some really dumb stuff. Breaking into little stores at night and, if they couldn't locate any money, trashing the shelves and making one merry mess out of what happened to be somebody's living.

These weren't poor kids either. Most of them came from decent homes and were raised by good people with enough money. Like the Hanneforts.

I don't know why Bucky Hannefort turned out the

way he did. He stole bikes, and then he busted into the Exxon station after some quick cash. He even slugged the old guy who was on night duty. I'd asked him why.

He told me. "For kicks, man."

Kicks?

Because I'd been half a block away, waiting for Bucky, the cops took me in. Both of us. I hadn't even known what Bucky was intending to do. All he'd said was, "Hang tough, Collin. I'll be back in a shake."

So I got busted.

The cops telephoned Dad, and he came down to the police station and got me. I told both the officers who picked me up that I didn't have anything to do with Bucky's caper. Maybe one of the cops believed me. The fat one sure didn't. And he wasn't too gentle as his partner read me my rights.

I hated it. But Bucky was smirking, as though he was some big-deal hood. All I could do was force myself not to cry.

It wouldn't have been so bad, except that the elderly man who worked nights at the Exxon station got his head cracked and went to the Greenwich Hospital. Worse yet, the old guy had to quit his job. Either that or he got fired because his boss figured he was too old to defend the cash drawer against a teen-age punk.

Closing my eyes, I imagined that I saw Mr. Kirk getting slugged by Bucky Hannefort. He fell, bleeding. On the pine bed, my entire body clenched, as if ready to fight. I sort of saw myself wade in, cock a fist, and punch Bucky out.

"Stop." I said the word aloud, trying to discipline my mind back into more reasonable channels. Why do I think so much? And do so little.

Funny, but I still like Bucky Hannefort, despite his dragging me into trouble that night. He really wasn't a bad kid, except that once. Maybe he just wanted some attention and chose a wrong way to get it. Well, he got it. His name was withheld in the Greenwich *Time,* but everybody in town knew. All he got was probation, in his parents' custody.

It wasn't enough. Bucky himself said so. I figured he was disappointed that he wasn't locked up.

Soon after, the Hanneforts moved to Chicago. And I never saw Bucky again. I wrote him a letter that he didn't bother to answer. Yet I knew it was the right thing to do, so I'm glad I wrote it. I told him in the letter to get a fresh start and to keep it fresh.

Nobody blamed me. Except *me.* That night, I probably should have guessed what Bucky was up to and tried to cool him before he headed toward the Exxon. Maybe he would have listened. Maybe not.

Rolling over on my bough bed, I tried to forget Bucky Hannefort and save my own neck.

Across the cabin, Mr. Kirk groaned on his cot. It made me wonder what his boyhood was like and what memories unfolded in his dreams.

My stomach growled in hunger. Back home, I used

to sneak downstairs around midnight, let the light from our refrigerator flood the darkened kitchen, and grab me some goodies. This was as close to crime as I ever got, a nocturnal icebox raid.

But I couldn't do it here. No way. My three-cents-a-day earnings didn't include eating more than my share, and for some reason, I didn't relish Mr. Kirk's going broke because of a minor hunger pang.

When a kid lives in Greenwich, I thought, he is one lucky kid. But at the time I didn't realize how lucky. Lying on my hip, I tried to picture what Mom and Dad ate for dinner. A big thick steak? Lamb chops? Plenty of mint jelly. I used to make myself a peanut-butter sandwich with mint jelly. Lots of it. Probably a lot more than three cents worth.

Can I really tough it out up here? Ah, quit thinking and go to sleep, Pepper.

13

"Snow."

Opening my eyes, I saw Sabbath Kirk standing in his underwear. One of his wool stockings had a hole that showed his big toe. He stood at the open door, looking out.

"It snowed in the night," he said. "Ground's white."

I didn't care if all of Vermont had turned pink or purple or vanished completely. My body was so sore that I knew I couldn't move. Yet my stomach was hollow enough to nag.

"What's for breakfast?"

"Don't know yet, 'cause it's your turn to cook."

"Me?"

"You. Can't be an eater the way you fork it all down 'less you learn to cook proper."

Attempting to sit up, I groaned. So did Tool, who had stayed indoors all night, sleeping under the old man's cot.

He looked at me. "What's the matter?"

"I ache all over."

"Well, if it'll loosen you up any to hear it, so do I. Cut more 'n a week's wood yesterday, you an' me."

"So today we can rest."

Mr. Kirk grunted. "Like fun. I'm sick to death of beans. Et 'em all winter, and it's near to spring."

Crawling up and out of my bedroll, I peered out the sink window. Vermont was white with fresh powder. The woods were quiet and still. I trembled. It all looked so cold through the crystal frost on the glass of the windowpane. And it was almost as dark outside the cabin as inside it.

"It's cold in here," I said.

"Don't whine about it. Stir the stove."

Lifting up a griddle of the Acme American, I looked inside at nothing except what appeared to be a gray bed of cold ashes.

"It went out."

"Nope. Only banked."

"What do you want me to do?"

"Twist the damper handle on the pipe. Poke up the ash, let some air under it, and she'll revive and dance up hot."

I did it. "Now what?"

"Soon's you blow some red coals, add a few twigs from the bottom of the woodbox. No, you durn fool, not the big ones. I said *twigs*."

"You sure wake up in a sugary mood."

"Morning's bad on me."

"Why?"

"Lame. I got me arthritis, and morn's the worst time. It's like the night turned me into marble."

Sabbath Kirk rubbed his stiff hands. Tool eyed him, possibly sensing that he was in pain. I heard her whine as though she could also feel his hurt. I wanted to pet her.

"Well," the old man snapped, "don't just stand there and stare. Fix us a meal."

"Out of what?" I asked.

"Is there anything hung back of the stove?"

I looked. "Yes, there's something here."

"What's it be?"

"One of your old socks. Do you want it baked, fried, or boiled?"

Kirk snorted. "Nothing else?"

"No."

"Shucks, I could of swore I'd dried some squirrel meat, but I must've . . ." He looked at the dog. "Tool, did you steal that there meat?"

Tool looked at the old man, and for a second I almost thought she was going to talk. And confess that she'd eaten the dried squirrel. If she had, I certainly owed her a favor, as I wasn't about to gag down some old hunk of squirrel. Nobody could ever get that hungry. Luroleen Bunkum called them tree rats.

"Well, boy, looks like it's going to be beans or corn bread again. I don't preference either one."

"Neither do I."

"So, we'll have ourselves the both."

"Mixed together?"

We ate the concoction, washing it down with hot mugs of my miserable coffee. I was grateful we had food. For the first time in my life, I was thankful for a meal. And without bowing my head or listening to some formal Thanksgiving Day blessing given by Dad, I felt blessed by what I ate.

We fed Tool the same meal, and she snapped it up. I was surprised. Back home, Winnie was so fussy and finicky, turning up her nose to Gravy Train one day and Chuck Wagon the next. And here was skinny old Tool eating anything and everything and darn glad to get it. Her tail said so.

It all made me wonder what Luroleen Bunkum fed her five kids. Boiled beans and corn bread? I remembered the many breakfasts that I had left half eaten on my mother's English bone-china plates. Crisp bacon, links of country sausage, waffles with maple syrup, and running butter. Tall glasses of orange juice and cold milk.

I said, "Good girl, Tool."

The dog looked at me with her silent brown eyes. How much do you know about me, Tool? I wondered. Do you know that I'm Collin Pepper from a well-to-do family in Greenwich? I bet you're not impressed.

Pulling on my shoe, I leaned forward.

"Don't touch her."

"I won't. I'd just like to know when I can pet her, that's all."

"She'll let you know when it's proper."

"How?"

"By coming to you. But don't you advance on her. Never. Let her approach you, and when she does, don't touch her even then."

"What should I do?"

"When the time comes, let her smell your hand and make all the moves. Once she does that, you'll be able to pet her and love her to your heart's content."

"I miss Winnie. She's my dog back home. But she never came to me very much either."

"Is that so?"

"Animals don't like me."

"You'll figure out why," said Kirk.

"I already have."

"And?"

"Maybe my father was right. Maybe I don't like *myself* a whole lot."

The old man pulled on his heavy coat. "Did you like yourself when you were falling asleep last night?"

"Sort of." I wondered how the old goat knew.

"Let me see your hands."

I showed him. "They're all blistered."

"Painful?"

"Yes, if you'd really care to know. I hope we aren't going to cut more wood today."

Muttering to himself, he emptied out several old coffee cans of junk until he found what he was searching for. A sewing needle. He stuck it in the fire and then cooled it in a dipper of water.

"What are you going to do?"

"Pop your blisters."

"Will it hurt?"

"Only if'n you let yourself be a baby and allow the hurt to fear your mind. Stretch out your paw."

He pricked the biggest blister, and water poured from it. It didn't hurt, even though I was sure it would. He went on to open the smaller bubbles on both my hands.

"There," he said finally. "Tool, we doctored up this here whelp real respectable. Nothing to it. Well, was he sturdy?"

Tool wagged her tail.

"Tug your coat on, boy." The old man reached for his shotgun. "We're going for meat, on account of me an' beans are near ready to go separate." He looked out the window.

"Are we going hunting?"

"Yup. I feel tracks out yonder. And it weren't no rabbit. No siree."

"Well, what was it?"

"A whitetail."

14

The snow was an inch deep.

Once outdoors, I saw Sabbath Kirk bend down and examine an animal track in the snow. To the east the sun was rising, and we could see more with every passing moment.

"What's a whitetail?" I wanted to ask, but I didn't. Kneeling down beside the old man, I looked at the track. It had been printed by a delicate hoof. There were two marks, both sharply pointed at the toe and round at the heel.

"Deer," I said with a considered guess. It wasn't a cow. That much I knew.

Mr. Kirk nodded.

"I thought you could hunt deer only in the fall. Now it's against the law. It's April."

Sabbath Kirk spat. "Law? The only law that counts is God's good hunger. All the rest can go squat."

I decided I wouldn't advise him further on legal matters. Not up here. Kirk was his own justice. Maybe that was what Dad meant when he'd told me I was going to law school. Well, I sure was learning. Still trying to hate every minute of it. As I stood, my spine hurt like fury, a harsh reminder of yesterday's saw.

Then I looked over my shoulder at all the wood I had piled, under Mr. Kirk's guidance. And I gave myself an A-plus. Yet I wished my body weren't so sore. All that ache for three cents.

Tool smelled the deer track. Then, looking at the old man, she waited for a command she appeared to know would follow.

"Deer," said Mr. Kirk to the dog. Glancing at me, he said, "She knows. Don't need you or me to tell this wise old girl." He stroked the dog's head. "Tool, go bring him to us, girl. Drive!" He slapped Tool's flank, and off she ran, fresh snow kicking up behind her rear paws.

"Come on, boy."

"To where?"

"You'll see." Cracking open the Purdey, the old man shoved in a green shell. "This here load contains one ball. It's a slug. A sixteen gauge is the best all-around gun an eating man could carry—for mice or moose."

"How will we ever catch up to a deer?"

"Won't bother to. Tool can circle down and drive him back our way. We'll wait our watch and sit patient."

"You'll have only one shot."

"Collin, your first shot is always your best. And on

deer, your first shot is usual your *only*. For my dough, a repeater rifle don't do much more than make extra holler. All second shots do is nick bark."

"I want to shoot the deer."

"And eat beans."

His insult angered me. "By that, I suppose you meant I'd miss."

"You probable would. I won't. Leastwise, that's what I usual tell myself. Now, we got ourselves one shot, just one ball twixt us and more beans, and I think I'm the one to take it."

"Where do we go to wait?"

"Them tracks is fresher than wet paint. We'll not wait long. Did you mark the droppings?"

"No, I didn't see any."

"I did. That deer dung was still steaming, hot from his bowel into cold snow. I felt the warm of it while you was priding your heart at the woodpile."

I shrugged.

We walked on farther through the soft powder. "You best learn to look ahead, lad, and not praise yourself too much on yesterday's doing, but rather on today's job."

"I will, Mr. Kirk."

"Yesterday's clean gone. We got wood to prove its worth. And your worth. But today's a deer day. So forget the saw and ax, plus all your muscle misery. I ache more 'n you do. Got cramps, too. Best we think about naught except to hunt the whitetail."

"I can't hear Tool anywhere."

"You won't. She'll work him our way by nostril. Tool can read wind and let that deer smell her just enough to make him shy away easy, instead of spooking him into a gallop that'll run right through our underwear before we even blink at the blur."

"Aren't you afraid of getting caught by the game warden?"

"Nope. I know the county game protector right well. He comes to my shack near about every time he gits lost." The old man cackled a laugh.

"Don't expect me to swallow all these tall tales you're always telling me. I don't believe *half* of it."

"If you had any brains, you simple whelp, you wouldn't believe *any* of it." Sabbath Kirk winked.

I was hoping the old rascal would trip on a root and blow his foot off, but no such luck. He probably had the Purdey on safety. Mr. Kirk was, I decided, a man who always was aware of what he was doing. Not to mention what people around him were thinking.

Well, maybe he was a big deal up here in Vermont, but nobody would even notice the old buzzard in Greenwich, Connecticut. Either that, or everyone would notice him. And laugh.

"This is it," he said quietly.

We stood in a patch of white birch. The trees were leafless and scratchy, more naked than the bristles on a hag's broom. The main trunks were blotchy white with twigs that were black and brittle. I snapped one.

"Is this where we wait?"

Kirk nodded. "Tool will come by."

"How soon?"

"May take her a minute or an hour. Tool works a deer at her own speed, and you don't hustle her. A dog knows what to do. Rest is up to the gun and the gunner."

He hunkered down at the base of a thick birch and motioned for me to do likewise. So I crouched, noticing the long knife that Mr. Kirk was wearing on his belt. It hung below the frayed edge of his colorless coat, peeking out like one old dragon tooth. The leather that covered the blade had weathered to a dry deep brown.

"Now hush, boy. Not a word from now forth. Don't even whisper."

"Okay," my lips said silently.

I listened, closing my eyes as Mr. Kirk was doing, straining to detect even the lightest of distant sounds. We waited, waited, and waited. I really hadn't intended to go back to sleep. It just happened. The roar of the Purdey practically stopped my heart!

Opening my eyes, I saw the old man up on his feet, running forward through the birch trees, and I heard Tool bark. Just once.

"Come on, boy."

Turning, he tossed me the heavy shotgun, which was still smoking, and I caught it, smarting my cold hands. The barrel metal was ice and iron. Ahead of us, I heard Tool again, snarling. And I heard thrashing in brush.

"Anchor him fast, Tool."

The old man's breath feathered out faster and faster into the cold air of a gray morning that was turning to gold and silver on the new snowfall. I could hear Mr. Kirk's lungs complain louder as he ran. The knife blade flashed from its sheath as we got to where the animal had fallen.

The deer kicked furiously at Tool, whose teeth held one of its rear legs. Dots of blood spattered the air, and the snow beneath the fallen whitetail was a circle of red slush. I didn't know the first thing to do except watch with an open mouth as Mr. Kirk threw himself on the deer. I saw a hoof strike Tool's head, yet she held the deer leg with her snarling jaws. Again the deer kicked her.

Shielding his face from the slashing antlers with one hand, the old man cut at the deer's throat. The knife missed. But the second thrust was followed by a gusher of steaming blood. The kicking of the deer's hooves softened until they were no more than a part of the dying of a trembling tan animal.

"Good girl, Tool."

The dog still gnawed the lean leg.

"Mr. Kirk?"

He gave me no answer.

"Mr. Kirk—I'm going to be sick."

Somehow I leaned the empty Purdey into the fork of a young tree, then stumbled forward on my knees, staring at the motionless brown eyes of the dying white-tail. The deer's eyes looked at me as though suddenly knowing now what a gunshot was, what a knife is, and what death would be.

The old man slapped a handful of wet snow into my face. It didn't help. I wanted to close my eyes and pretend it all had not happened. Only a bad dream. Mom would wake me up for school and kiss me.

Heaving, I threw up my beans and corn bread into the pools of bloody slush.

15

"Get up on your feet."

"I don't think I can do it."

The old man kicked at me. "Boy, right now, I don't give a hootin' geedee what you think. Fetch yourself up and help me hang the meat."

"I won't do it."

Kirk slapped my face with a wet and bony hand. "You either pitch in or you won't eat one scrap of it. Take your choice."

"God, I'm so sick."

He grunted. "Sick? You're damn healthy compared to this here dead animal. My leg got twisted, boy. And my dog's hurt. So stand up, grab yourself an antler, and heft. Or so help me Holy Hannah, I'll boot your backside from hell to supper."

Tool whimpered. Her right ear was deeply gashed, and blood ran down her coat into the white scarf of neck fur.

"Damn it, Collin," the old man growled at me, "it

don't take no brain to see that you're the only whole member here. My leg won't hold, Tool got herself hoofed to hurting, and the deer's deader than Adam."

"I don't think I can—"

"Tug!"

Eyes closed, smelling the sweet scent of blood and gagging on the sour stink of my own vomit, I yanked on the antler. The horn felt rough and pebbled in my hand. Mr. Kirk pulled beside me, his face twisting as he tried to favor one leg. I noticed that his hand seemed to want to grab at his belly.

"Snake off your belt."

"What for?"

"Hurry! Lash them antlers to a branch."

"Which one?"

He grunted. "Any damn limb you can reach up for and we can both bend down. Hang his rack high as you can stretch."

I did it. Somehow, gagging with every chore he barked at me, I helped him hang the dead animal. Kirk was breathing heavily. He sat, tossing me the knife.

"Skin him down."

"Me?"

"Yes, you, Mr. Big Eater. I would certain like to meet all the good folks who been butchering *your* meat for the last fifteen years. Or powdering your baby butt. Who in hell is this Collin Pepper kid? Are you some grand duke or holy emperor that got excused from all the dirt and duty?"

"No, it's just—"

"Ha, it's just my backside bottom. Are you one o' them vegetarians I heard tell about? You plan to graze out in the meadow with cows and nibble daisies?"

"No."

"Then you skin that animal and skin 'im sudden. Deer hide harbors lots of odor, and it'll taint our venison. Open the throat to cut out his windpipe before the neck meat sours."

"I'll try."

"More 'n that. Do it."

I skinned and gutted the deer.

The job took the morning, but I got it done, while Mr. Kirk sat with his wounded dog and twisted leg, watching every swipe of the knife. He told me where to cut, and I did the cutting. Several times, the blade punctured the intestines, and the putrid smell clouded me, flooding my nose and mouth with the stunning smell of dead excrement.

I didn't stop. But I did turn around once to toss Tool a scrap of what appeared to be a tender morsel of raw venison. It worried me when she sniffed it and refused. Slowly I peeled off the hot hide and emptied the body of all organs. The hardest part was removing the lower intestine and cutting out the anus. The waste finally lay steaming in the bloodied snow.

"I'm done."

"It took you long enough. Must be dang near August, and my meat'll spoil out rotten."

"That's not quite right, old man."

Sabbath Kirk squinted at me, still sitting. "How's all that go again?"

"It may be your deer, Mr. Kirk. And your gun, your slug, your dog, your blessed knife, and your whole bloody forest. But it's *my meat*."

"Is it now?"

"You bet it is. Half of it's mine to eat. And right now"—I wiped the sweat and blood from my face—"I swear I'd fight Loomis Broom to keep it. And I'd win."

Mr. Kirk raised both his eyebrows. "That so?"

"Yes, that's so, Mr. Wishbone Kirk. Right now, I hate the guts of this dead animal, but I hate your guts a whole lot worse. And you know what? I don't give a rat's tail what you think of me."

"You don't know what I think of you."

"And I don't care. But if you ever kick me again, for any reason"—I pointed the knife at him—"I'll skin out *your* windpipe so fast you won't even be able to rot a flea."

"Oh?"

"I'll chop wood. I'm willing to saw it, carry it, and help cook with it. And I'll help skin whatever we kill. But I'm not your servant, and I sure don't intend to be your football. Understand?"

"Yup." As he spoke, he held on to Tool, stroking her softly as though nothing was wrong. His other hand gripped his belly.

"I'm a person, Mr. Kirk. You may look at me and see just a dumb kid who's got lots of bucks and no sense, but I *am* a human being. I have feelings. And I can love *my* dog just as much as you love yours."

"I accept that."

"Winnie's just as good as Tool, because she's my dog and I love her. And I don't give a damn if Tool eats what I throw to her or starves to death."

"You all through?"

"No. There's one more thing."

"Like what?"

"I cooked our breakfast, so it's your turn to cook supper. And I won't eat beans. What I want is a deer steak. Venison, or whatever fancy name you give it." The momentary thought of eating the raw meat in front of me made me ill again. I gagged.

"Help me up, boy."

Leaning down, I let him hook one arm around my neck so I could help him to his feet. Tool lay on the ground.

"What'll we do with your dog?"

"Leave her here. She'll fetch herself home. If not, I reckon she's done for, and she'll die herself dead."

"No."

"Come on, boy. Let me lean on you."

"Not if you're going to leave Tool here."

"I know what's best for her. She's old."

"Too darn bad she's old. You're old, too. Do I leave *you* here? Well, I'd rather leave you here than leave her."

"You really care about her, don't you, boy? Even

though she doesn't care about you. Tool don't give a howl whether you live or die."

"Maybe not. But I want her to live." I looked at the deer carcass hanging behind me. "I've seen and smelled and carved up enough death for one day. I don't want anyone else to die."

"Not even me." The old face crinkled at me.

"No, not even you. Can you walk okay?"

"I can walk. If not, I'll limp or crawl. I got me a cramp, and my ankle hurts. It ain't serious. Don't feel nothing broke."

"What about Tool?"

"Leave her."

"No." I handed him the bloody knife and took two steps closer to where Tool was lying on the red snow. "She'll freeze to death out here."

"Don't touch her, boy. You do, and she'll snap away your throat before either you or I could whoa her."

"I don't believe you."

"You'd best do."

"Well, I don't." Turning to the dog, I spoke to her softly, looking at her torn ear and face. She had lost more blood, and her snout was sticky and shiny.

"Keep back," the old man warned.

"Tool," I said. "You're hurt, and I'm going to pick you up and carry you back to the cabin, where I can wash you clean and feed you. So bite me if you want to."

Slowly I reached out my hand and heard the growl that came from her throat.

"Why be a fool, boy?"

"Easy now, Tool. I won't hurt you. Good dog."

Even as she continued to growl, I touched her head, hoping that my hand would stop shaking. This wasn't Winnie I was touching. Tool was a Vermont dog, a mountain animal, a lot more wolf than poodle. Worse yet, she was *his* dog. She was bright, strong, lightning quick—and sorely wounded.

My hands slid beneath her, and I felt her hot body tremble. Her face winced, in pain or in temper. I saw the thin black lips curl back and the white teeth separate. Her jaws opened as I lifted her weight in my arms and held her against my chest. I stood up tall. Raising my face, I looked at the sky. She had my throat for a target. One snap and she could rip out my jugular.

I carried her home, praying with each snowy step. She was heavier than I had guessed, and my arms shook. The old man leaned the door open as I bore his dog into the welcoming warmth of the cabin.

Tool licked my face.

16

Mr. Kirk fell on his cot. He just curled up and lay there, so I asked him, "Are you badly hurt?"

"I ain't exactly fettle."

"You'll be okay." As I said it, I really hoped he would be, even though he'd turned into a cross old cuss.

Tool whimpered.

I had laid her down on my bedroll so she'd be comfortable. Kneeling beside her, I noticed that she lifted up the tip of her tail to show me a feeble wag. Just once.

"Easy now, girl."

Using an old sink cloth, I washed the caked blood off her face, hearing her low growl as I lightly touched her torn ear. The old man watched me, saying nothing. Lifting up Tool's ear, I was surprised by what I saw. It was a brand. The initials S.K. had been burned into the soft underside flap of the dog's ear.

While bathing Tool, I kept thinking about Winnie

—and home. Hoping that if my dog ever got hit by a car, somebody would care for her in a gentle way. And really *care* about her.

"The cut's deep, Mr. Kirk. Should I thread the needle and try to sew her up again?"

"Good idea—if you want your face tore off."

"Tool won't bite me now. No matter what I do to her."

Kirk snorted. "If'n that's what you want to believe."

"Then I'll do it."

"No."

"Why not?"

"Because there's no need. Animals got a way to heal up. Her wound needs to mend from the inside out. The deep'll heal first. During that time, the outside gash'll stay wet and runny. We only got to worry on Tool if we notice an early scab. Long as the surface wound is open, she'll fix."

I believed him. Maybe he wouldn't come right out and say so, but in his way he worried about Tool as much as anyone ever fretted for a dog. So I decided to ignore what came out of his mouth and judge what was in his heart.

"How's your leg?"

"Swelling."

"I'm sorry."

"An old goat like me shouldn't be rasslin' in the snow with a wounded forkhorn. Not if he's got any sense, which I don't. I'm feelin' real poorly."

"Tell me what to do and I'll do it."

"Would, if I knew."

As he spoke, his voice was softer. He grunted out his speech as if each word was being strained through a curtain of pain. The position of his body had also changed; he was lying curled on his cot, knees drawn up close to his chest. His hands circled around his knees and held on.

"Are you hungry?"

"Nope. I'm too grieved to fork food and too mean to starve. See to my dog. What's ailing me'll pass. All I got is a twisted leg and a cramp in my belly."

"A stomachache?"

"Sort of. It's your dang worthless cookery. That and all the time I had to wait in the cold while you hided off that deer an inch an hour."

"How fast were you the first time you had to skin a deer?"

"I forget. Long time ago."

"Yeah, I bet. How old are you anyhow?"

"Don't know and don't care. Plus it ain't any of your affair if I'm two hundred."

I crossed to his cot and sat down on the edge. My added weight rolled the sagging springs and made the old man wince. He yelped at me. "Get off, ya clumsy pup."

"I will. But first, let me look at your leg or your ankle or whatever it is that's hurting you."

"You ain't no doctor."

Sighing, I said, "No, but I took a course in school

on first aid. And my grandfather really is a doctor. Over the years, I've studied a good number of his medical books."

"You ought to take a study on keeping your young yap shut and leaving folks alone."

I touched his leg.

"Leave me be."

"Yeah, I know. If I try to help you, you'll bare your fangs and rip my throat out. Sorry, but you've already told me that story. I don't believe you, and neither does Tool."

"Don't pester me."

"Which leg is it?"

"Left."

Carefully I untied his boots, easing them off and throwing them under his cot where they joined his storehouse of dirty clothes. His socks were no joy. Had there been anything in my stomach it would surely have soared straight up. Lifting the frayed cuff of his left pant leg, I touched his white hairless skin.

"Your ankle's swelling."

"Told ya it was, didn't I? Ain't serious."

Going outside, I gathered up a pan of snow, came back inside, and ice-packed his leg, hearing his abuse and complaining during the entire process. Each time he swore at me, Tool growled, which didn't help much.

"Bed'll be sop. All that snow will melt. I'm cold enough. But my cussed gut sure ain't."

The fire in the Acme American was low, so I poked

it, shook down some ashes with the crank, and added some of yesterday's wood. Slowly the cabin warmed, but the heat began to smart my eyes. A strong smell.

"Ya dang idiot."

"You feel warmer, don't you?"

"What you did was stuff in green. The wood weren't seasoned ripe yet."

"Well, it's that or let you freeze. You probably got chilled out there, sitting on your buns in the snow while I did all the skinning and gutting. Watchers best not complain about workers."

I tucked him under his blankets, even though he continued to gripe about every move I made. Poking into his collection of coffee cans, I found some loose tea over which I poured some boiling water. As I handed him his white mug of steaming tea, he refused it.

"Drink it. It might warm up either your belly or your disposition, and I really don't care which one."

Snorting, he took the tea. After one incautious sip, he gulped a swallow, spat out the rest, and barked, "I'm scalded."

"Tough."

He was silent for several minutes. Then he apparently remembered something. "There's a meat saw in the corner." He pointed.

"You want me to cut off your leg?"

"No. Just stop asking tomfool questions, and hark. I want you to go back and section the deer, before them cussed coydogs come and there ain't nothing left."

"Coydogs?"

The old man nodded. "I seen tracks this morning. Tool smelled 'em. Saw more 'n just one set, too. Heard 'em howl in the night. You was asleep."

"Are they like wolves?"

"Ain't no wolves in Vermont. Saw one once, years back. Not recent. They all been shot or run north to Canada."

"Thank gosh."

"Coys can be near worse."

"How come?"

"A wolf'll steer clear of people. Don't favor humans any more than I do. But a coydog is a different breed."

"Is it like a coyote?"

"A Vermont coy'll balance forty pound. Shot one once that was near fifty. Bigger 'n old Tool by a whole lot. Run in packs, they do. Coy's just a wild dog and meaner 'n Moses."

"Will they see our meat?"

"Won't need to. A coy'll smell that fresh kill for ten mile away."

"Okay, I better get started." I took the meat saw from the corner and showed it to him. "Is this it?"

"Yup."

"How do I use it?"

"Stand facing the belly of the carcass. Saw down

between the legs—twice, once on each side of the backbone. Cut the neck clear off with a crosscut. Separate the shank from the round on each leg."

"I don't understand."

The old man winced. "Shank's the lower leg. Round is thigh. Rump's above that. Cut off loin and rib for roasts. Use my knife to strip the flank meat off the belly, which you then roll up cozy. Got it?"

"I can do it."

"Find some clean rags out back. They'll be stacked neat so take only what you need. Work quick or it'll be dark. Wrap each hunk of meat in cloth, fetch it back here, and pack it inside the smokehouse in snow. Ice, if you can find some that the noon sun melted. It'll be froze back by now. Bolt the shed door when you're done. Or them coys'll come and make it off."

"Anything else?" I started toward the door, looking back at him. He was holding his belly with both hands, and his face was twisted.

"Take the Purdey and shells. Light load."

"Is that all?"

"Wear your coat. I need you too bad for you to take sick on me."

I almost smiled at him as he almost smiled at me. Our eyes did. Carrying the Purdey and the saw, I ran out the door and grabbed the cloths, heading north to where we'd hung our deer, knowing the exact place it would be. The sun was deep to the west. Hurry, my mind warned me. Breathless, I trotted through the open stand of white birches, wondering how I'd cook the venison for our supper, hoping I could get both the old man and the dog to eat.

Then I stopped. Our deer was gone.

17

I swore.

There in the soiled snow lay the pile of organs I had gutted from the deer. Yet the branch wasn't entirely bare. My belt still hung there, knotted loosely about the limb. The buckle tinkled in the wind. I ripped the belt down, stuffing it into one of the big pockets of my heavy jacket and, for some reason, thinking of what would be for supper.

"Beans," I said.

Looking back up at the naked branch, I wondered how the coydogs could have jumped high enough to unfasten the knots around the antlers. I had tied them snugly. Nor was my belt broken. Snaking it out of my pocket, I examined my belt a second time. Still in one piece. And the leather was free of teeth marks.

The roar of a shotgun exploded in my mind with the sudden remembering of what had happened only two days ago. It was the bang of Loomis Broom's gun blasting the dead rabbit into nothing.

Because I had taken *his* meat, he . . .

Down on one knee, I searched the packed snow. Paw prints. They were all small. Everywhere, but all of one size. Dainty, and all Tool's. Coydogs would have left bigger ones. No coys.

There were boot prints, so many that it was difficult to tell whose feet had left them. Mine and the old man's, probably.

Then I saw it. A big footprint made by a very big man. I saw more, crossing mine. Feet twice the size of my own. Having just handled Mr. Kirk's boots, I knew that they had not left a print this large. Or this deep. The boot print had been stamped heavily into the slush; it filled with water and froze. I looked around further and finally spotted it—a trail of red drag marks in the snow, and more prints.

Loomis Broom was a big man. Either that or a small gorilla. Funny, but I didn't laugh. Looking at the heap of intestines, I began to wonder how much guts I had.

"Tool," I said, even though she was back at the shack, "I carried you home, didn't I?" Maybe I wasn't such a candy-ass.

It was all because of the rabbit. A moron could have figured that much. I had taken Loomis Broom's meat, and now he had come back to reclaim it. With interest.

I stood up still holding the cloths, the saw, and the shotgun, feeling my hands become wooden with cold. Why had I tossed out the lined gloves that Mom had so lovingly packed into one of my suitcases? Because I'm dumb, that's why, I answered myself. Because I am know-it-all Collin Pepper, who never listens or learns and will live his life a loser.

"I lost our deer."

Why had I been so eager to shotgun some furry little rabbit ahead of Broom's dog? What a monster. That dog didn't really look like one. It was probably a crocodile with its tail bobbed. No, its mouth was too big for a croc. Maybe it was some weird descendant of a Tyrannosaurus rex.

Why was I standing here? Because I didn't know what to do, that's why. How could I slink back to the cabin and tell Mr. Kirk that somebody, a big somebody, stole our deer?

"Mr. Kirk, sir, you'll get a kick out of this. Remember that deer you shot and I skinned? Well, some local prankster made off with it. Isn't that a gas? Who? you ask. Oh, my guess is that it had to be one of our neighborhood juvenile delinquents. Papers are full of it these days. Mrs. Broom always said that little Loomis was becoming a problem boy. Confused. She even nudged him into analysis. And, as it turned out, little Loomis isn't a kid anymore. He's grown up. Blossomed into a tree-ripened ape. Three hundred pounds but cute as a berry."

I laughed out loud.

Shrugging, I turned and started toward the shack, knowing what hell I'd catch from the old man. He'd warn me all over again about how I'd shot the rabbit and how dumb it was to cause trouble.

Try as I would, I couldn't stop laughing. Or talking aloud to myself.

"Hello? Mrs. Broom? This is Officer Collin Pepper of the Vermont Highway Patrol calling. It's about your son Loomis. Yes, I'm afraid he's muddled into a bit of shoplifting. He walked into a Ford dealer's and picked up a pickup. No, not a sex offense. A truck. We found it under his shirt."

Giggling, I fell down in the snow. I felt the teeth of the meat saw prick my hand, but my fingers seemed to be too cold to care.

Tears came.

I wondered, am I laughing or crying? A real pity I'm such a jerk. No wonder neither Greenwich High nor Kent Preparatory want me. I don't want me either. Maybe I can just lie here in the snow and die laughing.

With some people, everything they do turns into dirt. It flops and falls over. Like houses you build up out of a deck of playing cards. It just crumbles.

"Up yours, Loomis!"

I was still giggling as I pictured the next scene. Maybe the coydogs would parade in and be really ticked off that the deer meat was gone. So they'd eat me instead. So long, Wishbone.

"Hello. Mrs. Pepper? This is the Vermont Forest Ranger calling. I have good news for you. Your son

Collin has been devoured by dogs. Yes, he's finally been accepted by somebody."

My feet kicked in the air. My mind raced on.

How do I tell him? Do I just casually stroll through the door and announce that all our meat's gone? Brother! They ought to make a TV show out of this. A sitcom. Just sit and be calm. When something goes wrong, you just fall down laughing into the snow and rip your hand on a saw. Old saws are never amusing.

"Hear that, saw? You're not funny anymore. Just rusty. Got fooled, eh? Thought you were going to sink your teeth into fresh venison. But old Loomis beat you to the rabbit punch. Hello? Mrs. Broom? It's about your son Loomis. This is Mrs. Rabbit calling, and I'm just wondering if your boy has been playing with my boy. He's been missing since day before yesterday."

Lord, what was I doing, thinking about a dead rabbit? I stopped my imaginings, rolled over, and lay face down, feeling the cold snow begin to burn my cheek.

Hey, I thought. Better not get the Purdey wet, or the old man will skin me alive. But not if I keep his knife!

Sitting up, I used one of the clean rags to wipe off the shotgun. I didn't even know why I was doing it. Maybe I was ready to tackle anything in order to delay my return to the cabin and having to stare old Kirk in the eye and tell him.

I could lie. Maybe if I told him that coydogs took the meat, there would be less trouble. But if he knew

Loomis Broom stole it, which I'm not even sure of, he might fly into a rage. Have a heart attack. Or maybe only swear at me instead of his constipation.

Maybe the old guy is sicker than he lets on. He says no bone is broken so the swelling is bound to subside. But the cramps? He did squat down in the snow for a long time, holding Tool. And he probably did catch one devil of a chill.

I kept wiping the Purdey. Now it was bone dry, but I kept working the rag up and down, around the steel barrel. I'd done enough wrong. Laughed when I should have cried. Wasted precious time on doctoring when I could have returned to hack up the venison. Now it was gone.

How do people who live up in these mountains ever begin to cope with crime? I wondered. Who do they turn to to right a wrong? Where's the law? I guess there isn't any up here. Except for the laws you pass yourself, sort of like the commandments. Thou shalt not gun down game ahead of another man's dog.

Laugh if you will, Pepper. What may be a joke to you is deadly serious to a Kirk or a Broom and to the rest. Serious and deadly.

I began to worry if my rabbit-hunting would spawn continued trouble for the old man. Would the theft of the deer end it? Or fan its fury? Do the mountain people in Vermont have feuds, like the infamous Hatfields and McCoys?

McCoys are sons of coys. Hey, that's good. But the McCoys don't even know they're sons of bitches.

Maybe the Hatfields tripped over the pun and started kidding the McCoys about it, and then somebody iced somebody.

I walked slowly, carrying everything, deciding what I'd do and when I'd do it, even if Mr. Kirk was going to object. Tough if he did. I was the boss now. He was old and sick and sore-legged. And I had his knife and gun. So there wasn't much he could do to stop the feud I intended to start, a feud that might even make history. I smiled.

Collin Pepper against the Brooms.

18

"She's still bleeding," I said.

The old man looked at Tool and me. "Good. It'll flush out her wound. Lost blood usual looks to be more 'n it is."

Mr. Kirk was still lying on his side on his cot, curled up in a ball, both knees jackknifed into his chest. He had not moved since I left the cabin. Watching him, I petted Tool.

"You brought in the meat?"

Not knowing how to answer him, I lied a truth. "We'll be eating venison almost as soon—as I learn to roast it."

"I ain't hungry."

Jumping on his remark, I said, "Okay, we'll just have corn bread or beans. Both or neither. I'm not very hungry either. By the way, is it customary for hunters to eat venison on the same day that it's shot?"

"Nope, not usual. Meat's like fruit. Gotta ripen. So

let it set and season a bit out back, and tomorrow night we'll have ourselves at it."

"Okay."

"If my gut quits kicking."

I sat on the floor, stroking Tool with a very light and gentle touch. "How do you feel, Mr. Kirk? Any better?"

"Poorly."

"Tool's cuts are still open. Here's a deep one on her body. Maybe I ought to thread our needle and sew her up, if I can."

"You can't sew a dog. I told ya that."

"Why not?"

"Lots of reasons. One, she might not allow it. Two, thread'll snap. Three, even if'n you was to sew up a dog with *gut*, the dog'll usual worry the stitches. Claw 'em or bite 'em broke."

"No. I'd wrap her up so she couldn't chew at them."

"S'pose. However, I'd just let Tool be, and permit her to heal lonesome. She's a tough old mutt. She'll mend."

"I wonder if she's hungry."

The old man grunted. "Nope. No wounded animal is. I ain't either. Are you?"

I shook my head. "No, sir, I'm not. Too much has happened today for me to even dream about food." This was no time for me to blurt out my confession about our stolen meat. And even if the venison was ripened, cooked, and on our table, I wouldn't have been able to force down one swallow. My belly hurt from throwing up.

Getting up, I checked the Acme American to see how our fire was holding. Carefully, I added what I judged to be the most seasoned wood I could locate, so the heat wouldn't smart our eyes as badly as it had earlier.

The old man groaned on his cot. His eyes were shut tight, and his body trembled beneath the army blanket.

"Do you have any brandy?"

"Yup."

"Where do you keep it? Hidden, I suppose."

"None of your business, 'cause you ain't going to drink any. I don't intend to shelter a drunken underage."

"It isn't for me. If you caught yourself a chill, the brandy just might help you ward off pneumonia or whatever your sickness could turn into."

"I'll mend." His voice was straining.

"I hope so."

Mr. Kirk snorted. "A lot you'd bother."

"You're not being a very cooperative patient. All you do is swear, groan, complain, and tell me that everything I do is dumb."

"My dang gut is cramped up so tight I plumb forgot my leg. Hurts like Hades."

I walked to the cot, leaned down, and touched the old man's face. "You may have a chill, Mr. Kirk, but you're burning hot." His forehead was very warm and clammy, with far more flush to it than could usually be seen.

"You put too much fool wood in the stove."

"Anything else?"

"Clean the gun. And make sure you tend to the meat saw. You likely hung it up wet and bloody. If so, the blade'll rust over."

There wasn't any meat to saw, I wanted to yell at him. None. Nothing but a frozen pile of entrails. But I got my belt back. I'm going to cook it for supper. Boiled belt, a specialty of the house.

Pulling my belt from my pocket, I threaded it through my trouser loops. I tightened it a notch. Days like today weren't too helpful for gaining weight. At least my pants won't drop down, even if my pounds do.

"Is it dark?" asked Mr. Kirk.

At the sink, I looked out the window. Against the darkened woods and sky, the snow gleamed a bluish white. At least there was no blood on this snow. I'd had my fill of gore.

"Yes, it's evening."

Looking at him, I wondered if the old-timer had any inkling as to what I was planning to do. I had lied, telling him that the meat had been cut up and treasured away. Not that I'd actually said it, but that's what he believed. So I hoped.

I thought about my plan. I would wait until he slept. Then I'd do what had to be done. Loomis, and all the Brooms in Vermont, were not going to get away with ripping off our game. No way. My face tightened. Pepper, I was thinking, you sure are one big talker, considering the fact that you're nothing but a lousy loser. Now I'd lost our deer. But I could steal it back again.

Closing my eyes, I could picture Loomis Broom and his gun, plus his big black dog. Why would anyone blow a dead rabbit into bits? Maybe the guy was a mental case. Like me.

"Hello? Mrs. Broom?" No, I thought, I'm not going off on that kick again. It's best I try to stay rational. Yet here I am, about to scoot off and possibly commit the stupidest act any kid ever took a swing at.

Bending down, I lightly petted Tool once more. Her eyes were so soft and such a deep brown. She was hurt herself, and possibly in pain because she knew that the old man on the cot felt pain.

"Good girl, Tool."

Her tail twitched. She knew me as a friend now. She had let me carry her when she was cut and bleeding. Resting my fingertips close to her nose, I waited for her to smell me, which she did. Her nostrils worked to widen and then to narrow as she inhaled my nearness.

"I hope you like me, Tool, because I like you."

"She likes ya."

Twisting my head, I looked at Mr. Kirk. He had kicked off his blankets and was straining to sit up.

"I gotta go out." His voice seemed to be in pain.

"Why?" I asked him.

"Best I go check the meat."

I felt my whole body sweat. Every pore.

"The meat is okay right where it is for now," I told him. "The time has come for you to trust me. Okay, you're still the boss. But let me do *one* chore around the place without you peeking over my shoulder."

His bare white feet touched the floor.

"You're not going outside, Mr. Kirk." I shot a quick glance at the dog and then looked at him. "Even old Tool is bright enough to admit she's ill, so you better stay in bed. I mean it."

"Stay put?"

"Right."

He hesitated, staring at me. "And leave you to look after matters like a growed man?"

I nodded.

His face contorted. The old guy was really hurting somewhere. Maybe he was wrong. His leg could have been fractured, and he wasn't aware of it. It made me wonder if he had, in his entire life, ever bothered to have a physical checkup. Or even met face to face with a doctor. I was wishing Grandfather were here.

"Your face is beet red," I told him.

"I know, boy. I can feel the blush of it."

"Lie down, please. You're going to mess around and make yourself worse. I'm right here, Mr. Kirk. And *blush* is hardly the word to describe your face. Try *burn*."

He looked at the stove.

Damn him. "Yeah, I know it, so don't bother to

repeat yourself. I put too much wood in the stove, and that's why your face is flaming with fever."

"I need a drink."

"Brandy?"

"No. Fetch me a dipper of water."

He drank it all. I drew him another, and again he drained the dipper.

"Thanks. That water's stale. Go out and fetch in some fresh. I hate warm water."

"Lie down and sleep. Here, I'll cover you up."

"I'm boiling hot, ya fool."

"Sure, and half of it is bad temper. I'm a spoiled brat, and you're a long ways from good-natured. Do you want some sort of a pillow under your head?"

"No. I just crave some quiet."

"Then be still. Most of the racket around here is blowing out of your own mean mouth."

He snorted and closed his eyes. I was hoping that the water would cool him enough to bring sleep, and soon it did. He snored worse than a saw. I petted Tool once more. Her eyes also drooped. After loading the Purdey, instead of cleaning it, I strapped the knife into my belt and blew out the candle.

I trotted north, hearing my boots squeak warnings on the powdery snow.

19

I thanked God for the moon. It was beautiful, like the War Head. It seemed to be pasted among the stars like a giant wafer. Silver, cold, white, and bright, it sparkled the snow crystals that had earlier thawed and were now refrozen. Ice crunched as I walked on the crust.

Following the trail was easy. No one is going to carry a dead deer. Not even a man the size of Loomis. Where did the Brooms live? Well, I would soon know. The dragging away of our whitetail left a path that an imbecile could pursue. I smiled, because Collin Pepper was the imbecile in pursuit.

"Here I come, Loomis," I whispered into the north wind. "And I sure hope you and your kin go to bed early."

The trail I followed through the woods became less and less bloody. Yet the big boots and dragged meat continued ahead of me like a road to nowhere.

No need to look at the sky or to mark the trail with tree notches. I was on a freeway. Looking down at the telltale route the thief had left, I remembered the Christmas I had been given a toboggan. The track was similar in width. An endless white snake of crushed snow, punctuated every yard by the sharper prints made by big boots. As he had pulled, his toes had dug deeper into the crust.

The drag of the meat failed to wipe the boot marks away. They were always there, every yard. Yet never alone. Paw prints of the big dog were there, too. They were almost twice the size of the tracks left by Tool's paws—just as the boots of Loomis Broom doubled mine.

My hands were getting cold, so I shifted the Purdey into the crook of my arm and jammed my fists into the pockets that slashed my jacket.

"Brr," I said.

How far away did Loomis live? A mile, two miles, five, ten, fifteen, twenty? I began to count his boot tracks. Reaching a hundred, I started over and reached it again and again, losing the tally in the night and the cold.

"Loomis," I muttered, "where are you taking this deer, to Canada?"

Ahead of me in the darkness, I imagined that I could see him. He was leaning forward, straining, one fist gripping one antler just below the budding fork. I saw Loomis Broom yanking, tugging, complaining about the weight of the meat. And, though I could not picture his face, he wore a cold smirk, because he was getting his revenge for the rabbit.

He was besting Sabbath Kirk.

No, big boy, I thought. No way. Because Kirk's hired flunky is coming to get you. You'd better be on guard, Loomis, if Collin Richardson Pepper is behind your back.

How many more miles? Just as I was walking and wondering, I noticed where Broom had stopped dragging the deer and had sat on a log to rest. Some of the snow had rubbed off its crest, exposing the black bark beneath.

Seeing it made me want to rest, too. I sat where he had sat. Today sure had been one killer of a day. What would tonight bring? Would I bring home the bacon? The thought made me snicker.

"Collin," my dad usually said about a thousand times every weekend, "the trouble with you is that you'll never learn to take life seriously."

"Hello? Dad? I'm calling from Vermont, long distance. No, I'm not in jail, and I'm not in the hospital, but that last may be only a matter of time. You see, Dad, you'll never guess what I'm doing. I've decided to turn private eye and track down a deer thief. Who? Oh, just Loomis Broom, some puny little punk who looks like he'd eat somebody's face."

I couldn't get myself to laugh. Except once, when I started thinking of Mr. Broom as the Incredible

Loomis. That broke the ice. Giggling, I almost tumbled off the log.

"On your feet, Pepper," I told myself.

The Purdey was getting heavier. Why had I never done any of those push-ups that coaches and fathers keep ordering boys to do? Why hadn't I jogged?

"You're soft, Pepper." I could hear the remark our P.E. instructor at Kent was yelling at me. "Give me ten, Pepper." That meant I had to flop to the turf and do ten push-ups. But I couldn't do ten. Eight was my record. The Incredible Me.

What was that big fink's name? Yeah, I recall. That old P.E. instructor's name was Horace Huntington. Kids called him Hunt the Grunt. Built like a bale of barbed wire and almost as pleasant. Well, I guess if your folks named you Horace, you sort of had to take push-ups seriously.

I followed the dragging trail.

Maybe, I was thinking, if Mom and Dad had named me Horace Pepper, I'd be one shimmering success. Names have a lot to do with it. How could a kid fail to become a hero with a name like Bart Starr? Josh Witten had Bart's autograph.

Breaking into a steady trot, I remembered all the running that people had tried to make me do. What a bore. If Horace Huntington had a god, it was Mercury, with winged feet. Mine were webbed. My god should be Daffy Duck. No. My god is the War Head. Beyond the sky.

Images of the Kent athletic field kept invading my brain as I ran, and I could hear the rasping voice of Hunt the Grunt yelling at me, singling me out as a loser. "Okay, Pepper, give me a lap!"

There had been that day in the Kent library when I'd accidentally knocked some dumb geography book off a table. It had fallen open, showing pictures of Scandinavian people all dressed in fur. So I tore out a photo of a Laplander, took it to gym class, and dogged it lazy on purpose. Then, when The Grunt yelled at me to give him a lap, I yanked out the picture and handed it to him.

"Okay," I'd said, "here's your Lapp."

Well, dear Horace, you ought to see Pepper tonight. Bet if you could, you'd fall over in a faint—which is just about how I feel right now.

Do I need the Purdey? The thought hit me that I wasn't really intending to shoot anybody. Not even lovable old Loomis. How, in the name of heaven, was I ever going to pack mule all the meat back to Kirk's place and still carry the gun?

I'm a fool, I thought. Everybody's right about me. They really do have Collin Pepper pegged. I can't find my butt with both hands. Wrong, I can. What's more, I can find Broom Manor and snatch back our deer carcass and bring it home.

Home? Wow, am I that far gone? I must be off the deep end and around the bend if I start imagining Kirk's musty old shack is home. Yet it is, for now. So I'm going to do what begs doing. Yuck, my words are even starting to sound like the old man's. I'm beginning to talk Vermont.

Stopping, I looked south, back toward the shack that was now miles away. I hoped Sabbath Kirk and Tool were both sleeping. Dreaming of roast venison instead of beans. I hoped I'd never see another bean.

"Purdey," I said, "you may not approve of this, but I'm parking you here. Right here, gun. And I'll pick you up on the way back."

Leaning the shotgun against a tree, I pulled some brush closer to hide it. Mr. Kirk would have a cow if I lost it. Pulling a soiled hanky from my pocket, I tied it to a twig, less than ten feet from the gun's nook. Wow, did I have smarts.

Feeling free, I trotted again. Faster, now that I was unburdened. The knife still rode my hip, and it felt comforting against my belt.

How much farther? I wondered. Where did these Brooms live, up at the North Pole? Maybe I could slow down a bit. Pace myself. After all, when I suddenly stumbled onto Loomis Broom's cabin, I really couldn't accomplish too much until they were all tucked into bed.

I thought of his dog.

Should I go back for the Purdey? No. Firing my shotgun wouldn't advance my cause. Besides, as I'd said earlier to Sabbath Kirk, there had been enough death for one day. But maybe the dying wasn't over.

Kids my age don't think about death. Or even talk about dying. When you're fifteen, you're immortal.

Death is too far down the long road. Too distant.
Maybe that's what the deer thought, up until the roar
of the Purdey. Then he felt that one lead ball of heat
rip through his body, smashing bones and puncturing
organs. I remembered removing one organ in particular. The liver had been in tatters.

A dog barked.

Sweat flooded me as I paused to listen. I had gotten there. Broom's place, or somebody's place, was in
front of me. Within earshot. Moving ahead with
hushed steps, I followed the tracks that led to louder
barking.

The trail twisted to a clearing and a cabin, inside
which a lantern burned yellow. I saw it through an
open doorway. A man stood there, ordering the dog to
still its barks. He threw something at the dog and
closed the door.

For only an instant had I seen the man silhouetted
black in the yellow door frame. Yet I knew him.

Loomis Broom.

20

I waited.

Why am I panting harder now than when I was running? I wondered. Because I'm scared out of my skull, that's why.

Kneeling in the snow, I unzipped to empty my bladder. At least I tried to, but I couldn't go. Cold bit into my kneecaps as I kept straining. Nothing happened. My clothes still smelled strong and felt stiff from my earlier disaster. Yet that was now a minor worry.

I kept hearing the same odd sound. A dull thud. Seconds would then elapse, and I heard it again, over and over. Moving closer, I discovered its cause—the dog.

He was tied by a rope that ran from his furry black neck about twenty feet to a post at a corner of the shack. When the dog charged again, the rope straightened with another thud. The shock must have

almost crippled his neck, yet he kept it up in an effort
to break free.

Finally the door opened, and I heard voices. I saw
and heard a different man speak to the black dog.

"What's that, boy?"

From inside the cabin, a female voice answered the
man at the door. "He's got wind of the meat, hanging
back, so he's trying to bust loose and eat sick."

"Bring the dog in, Clarence. And shut the dang
door les' we all freeze. Hear? And do sudden."

The man called Clarence untied the dog, and both
disappeared inside the shack, banging the door. Somewhere, off to my left, I heard the sleepy clucking of
some chickens, as if annoyed that their rest had been
so repeatedly disturbed.

A softness kissed my face. Looking up with a quick
flinch, I saw that the moon had faded into fuzz with
no stars. It was snowing. Big, lacy flakes danced toward
me. One here, one up there. Only a few. A large flake
hit my nose and melted.

An argument sounded from inside the shack. One
of the Brooms threw a pot or a pan at another, which
seemed to terminate the disagreement. I could hear a
woman's voice commanding their return to order.

The big black dog yelped out one big black bark
and then became mute. Hearing him made me grateful that he had been let in. But he was no longer on
a rope. One swing of the shack's door and the dog
would roar out into the night to defend his territory. I

was on Broom turf now, and the black dog would surely guard every inch and each ounce of what he knew was his.

I'd bet that dog's name wasn't Winnie the Poodle.

So, the deer meat was hung at the rear of Broom's shack. Then I'd find it. Not just now, but as soon as a Broom hand snuffed the lantern.

My spine shivered. Cold or fear? Both, I reasoned. Yet I was not as afraid as I had been earlier. Holding out my bare hand, I could see that my fingers were steady. Probably frozen.

The lantern died. Its yellow faded into purple and black and stillness. Someone inside pulled a big boot off a big foot and dropped it; then another. I continued to wait until I would be sure that all the Brooms were sleeping. Hopefully undressed. I had heard women inside, so there was a possibility of nightly activity to occupy the attentions of Broom males. Yet there remained the probability that Broom guns were kept loaded.

I heard no children. Maybe the young had already been stuffed away in their bunks.

My foot tested a step. Promising that I would consider each footfall, I moved closer by about eight or ten feet. Hearing talk, I stopped quickly, then to hear it no more. Again I moved, widely circling the shack, creeping through shadows until I was within half a stone's throw to the north side. There hung the deer. Still and maroon.

I wanted to be sure of my route to it. Brushing snow from my face, I worked forward keeping my body in a low crouch, feeling the twist of the knife sheath with each short stride of my folded legs.

Dare I do it? I asked myself. Do I have the guts to walk up to the shack and steal Loomis Broom's food? You bet your candy-ass I do. Because it isn't his deer. It's ours.

Looking at the cold red meat, hanging raw and furless, I wasn't hungry for it. But I wanted that venison for Sabbath Kirk.

A day ago, the old man had shown me dried deer gut, telling me that it had been used by Indians to string their hunting bows. And now I saw more of it. Tight knots of deer gut bound the antlers to a rafter that extended outward from a shed. My fingers fought the knots.

I remembered the knife. Easing it up from its leather sheath, I began to saw at the deer gut. But the blade screamed at it. A low voice muttered from inside the dark shack. I waited—counted to two hundred and then pressed my knife once more against the dried gut. The same sound cried out worse than a frantic fiddle. In less than a minute I realized I couldn't slice the bindings without blowing the whole caper.

The only thing that might be cut would be the skinny neck of Collin Pepper.

"Damn!" I muttered. Am I licked?

That's it, kid, I thought. Be sure you're a quitter.

Give up. Throw in the sponge. Have your mother line your bureau drawers with paper.

No, I won't quit, I determined. Mr. Kirk, I am bringing home our meat, so sleep away. And you sleep, Tool. Food's on the way. It may not be venison, but by darn, there's going to be meat on our table.

Even while I thought this, I took three more squeaky gashes at the deer gut with my knife. To no avail.

Careful, I warned myself.

Retreating from the hung carcass, I edged along the crunchy snow toward the westerly side of the shack, trying not to trip over litter and trash. The Brooms weren't too tidy. Stuff was thrown all over. Compared to them, Mr. Kirk was a paragon of neatness and order. Except for under his cot.

Thinking about him, I smiled. A lot he'd said made sense now. He was an okay guy.

As I approached one of the shabby outbuildings, I lifted the latch and slowly opened the door, surprising myself that I could be so deathly quiet.

All the hens were asleep.

Reaching out with both hands at once, I let my fingers encircle the necks of two of the nearest hens. Only one of them let out a squawk. But once was enough. In a second, every chicken in Vermont seemed to be screaming. Without closing the door, I bolted from the hen house and fled into the bushes with several hens fluttering after me.

Hearing the dog roar, I ran through the brush. It was snowing harder, and I couldn't see too well in the dark.

A voice hollered out. "Git the gun!"

"Hens is loose, Clarence. Must be a fox. Or coys. See if'n the deer's took."

I could still faintly hear the clatter behind me. The dog was loose, barking, causing the hens to panic. One of the Brooms accused another of not bolting the hen-house door.

As the two hens kicked and flapped, my fingers tightened on their necks. I dodged through the trees and falling snow, not knowing which way to head. The trail had disappeared. It had melted into the snowy night.

Why had I spent so much time hacking away at the deer meat?

"Come on, Pepper. Use your stupid brain. You've got to find those tracks."

Eyeing the ground, I sure was making enough footprints of my own. The hens still fought. I watched snowflakes and chicken feathers flutter to the white ground.

The dog barked behind me. Yet he didn't sound any closer.

Wet and puffing, I kept on running, trying to circle to my left and pick up the trail made by the dragged deer.

Thorns cut my face, forcing me to stop and ease myself out of the nest of long barbed canes. My cheek smarted. I wanted to loosen my hold on the necks of the two hens, but I didn't dare. If one of them squawked again, I'd be found for sure. Maybe the dog was already coming.

I guessed that with the falling snow there would be little scent to follow. Luckily, the confusion back at the Brooms' cabin was multiple—people yelling, the hens all escaping and creating a loud fuss, plus the strong smell of the hanging venison to divert the dog. I hadn't done too fancy a job of butchery. My meat did not at all bring to mind the carefully wrapped meat cuts at a supermarket.

The snow quickened. Smaller flakes now fell, but there were far more of them. They continued to pelt my face whenever I looked at a sky that promised nothing but winter. Whoever the songwriter was who wrote "April in Paris," my mother's favorite song, he never saw April in Vermont.

I'm lost, I finally admitted. In more ways than one.

Here I am, lost in a forest snowstorm, remembering old songs. My mind's blown.

I tried to calm myself. Hang on, Pepper, and force your brain to reason. Don't run. Reason. There has to be a wisp of logic in this dilemma. What do people do when they're lost in the woods? Classic answer— they walk in a circle. Now, that's exactly what I want to do, so eventually I will cross the trail that I followed here, and retrace it.

So I walked, carrying my two strangled chickens, wondering if my fingers were going to freeze. On and

on, among trees that all looked like cousins, imagining
that there was a Broom lurking beyond each trunk. Or
their delightful dog. I wanted to yell for help, but I
was too afraid of who might hear.

I almost cried when I saw it—my handkerchief,
fluttering on its twig like a brave little banner.

21

After ripping down my flag, I located the Purdey. It was exactly where I had hidden it and hadn't budged. But I would have to remember it was loaded. I hurried, as the trail that had been dragged by Loomis Broom was rapidly becoming hidden by the falling snow.

"Keep your head down, Pepper." Maybe if I talk to myself, I'll go bananas, but it sure beats freezing to death, I thought.

Keeping my eyes on the ground, I toted the Purdey in my left hand and one leg of each dead hen in my right. The gun was heavier than my pair of fowl. Strange, how I had already begun to think of the two hens as *mine*.

"They aren't yours, Pepper. You stole them an hour ago. Remember?"

I sure did. I just walked up, bold as you please, and ripped off Loomis Broom. That, I had to admit, was a boast few folks would dare to utter.

"Law," my father had said. I was up here in Vermont to learn law.

"Dad, I'm learning it real fast."

There are no laws in a wilderness. Well, maybe a few casual courtesies involving rabbits ahead of other people's dogs—but nothing much more formal. I was carrying my law. Eye for an eye. Two hens for one deer. It wasn't a real smasher of a swap, but then don't ignore the busted bunny. That, according to his law, belonged to old Loomis. So, I thought as I trotted along, that's how it all sums up. A rabbit plus two hens equals one poorly dressed deer. That, for tonight, is the local rate of exchange.

"Loomis," I said aloud, "it's a deal, baby." And I laughed at my new role as horse trader. Or was it rabbit-deer-hen trader? That's the spirit, Collin, I told myself. Don't lose your sense of humor. And *don't* take all this seriously because it isn't. It's only serious if you don't watch where you're going and get lost. You've got to think and remember and mentally mark every tree.

I felt I was going south. I'd bet my life on it. Maybe I *was* betting my life. Crap shooting it all on one reckless roll.

Hey, it's Collin Pepper, folks, I announced silently. The big shooter from Vegas. Poker player. Gambler. Just look at all his blue chips piled up on that green cloth. The pot is now swollen, and yet Pepper tosses in one more bank-buster of a bid.

"I'll see your deer, mister, and raise you two hens and a rabbit."

While chuckling at my own wit, I nearly let my stiff fingers drop the Purdey. Then my heart about leaped out of my shirt! I was passing the log where Loomis had rested, going home, and where I had also sat.

Aha! I shouted silently. I'm dead on due south. Wouldn't it be a holler and a half if I was the explorer who finally discovered that Vermont doesn't really have a north or a south. All the natives use is thisaway and thataway. Boy, my legs are tired. No, don't stop and don't sit. Give me a lap, Pepper. Just one more.

Passing the place, among all the white birch trees, where Mr. Kirk had killed the deer, I let out a whoop. I saw the branch we'd hung our meat on, using my belt, and waved a chicken at it.

I did it! I thought unbelievingly. I did it! Hear that, Josh? How about that, Horace? Look at me and grunt. If only Mom and Dad and Winnie were here, just the other side of the finish line, to cheer me home. I know what. While I was gone, old Kirk jumped off his cot and hired a brass band to herald my return. I looked up. Is that snow or confetti coming down?

I could see better. My eyes were growing accustomed to the night. I was becoming an owl. Every tree and rock looked familiar. And I could smell the cool green breath of pine.

The snow seemed to be letting up. Yet I still couldn't see any stars. Not a one. Mom used to sit at our piano, playing and singing all her square melodies. I could just hear her playing "I Only Have Eyes for You."

Oh, sweet Jesus, and I'm not swearing but praying, how I would love to hear Mom's piano right now. "Mom! Dad! Winnie!" Yelling as I ran toward the shack, my nose picked up a burning of green wood. Yet it wasn't a smell. It was fragrance.

"Mr. Kirk!"

I almost broke in the door. Bent over and crooked, he was standing at the sink, looking out the window, his back to me. There was no morning candle lit. But I could see it all.

Without turning, the old man spoke. "You up already?"

It stopped me. I hung the Purdey on its pegs and threw the dead hens outside before shutting the door. I almost fell before taking even one more step as far as the center of the cabin. And then I asked one of my usual witless questions.

"What time is it?"

Kirk grunted. "Morning."

It all hit me—why I had so suddenly been able to see in the dark. Mr. Kirk had slept all night. He didn't realize that I'd been gone from sundown to sunup.

Where? he'd ask.

Oh, I'd answer, just took a stroll over to Brother Broom's for a bite of chicken. It's only a million miles through a snowstorm. And I can find my way through Vermont woods like I was raised here. I kept my head and neither yelled nor flipped into a panic.

I fell down on my bedroll.

"You sick?"

"No," I told him. "Only dead."

"How come you're going back to bed? Decent folks get up in the morning, so best you do the same. Give me a good day's work and maybe we'll fix ourselves a venison steak for supper."

"And maybe we won't."

As I lay on my bedroll, I saw his body stiffen and his hands grab the edge of the sink. Had I not jumped up, he would have keeled over on the floor. Or maybe fallen into the stove.

He felt frail and hot. The light was becoming stronger because of the dawn, so I got a close look at his face. Burning red; and when I touched it, burning hot. Worse than that, all of his features—eyes, nose, mouth—were warped into a grimace of agony.

"What's wrong?"

"Cramps."

"Gee, I thought you were better when I saw you were up and around."

Easing him back to his cot, I could feel the heat of his body. He was a human Acme American, a stove, hot all over. He had not gotten dressed and was still in his long gray underwear. I wondered if it was his only undergarment, which he wore all winter. Probably was.

Inspecting his leg, I could tell that the swelling was still present. But the ankle trouble was not, he had told me, the chief source of discomfort.

"Where are your cramps? All over?"

"At my gut." His voice no longer spoke in its customary growl. His words were softer now, more distant. He was here in the cabin and yet going away.

Sabbath Kirk gasped for breath.

As he did, Tool whined. She was still lying in the same warm place where I had left her, near the stove. Her brown eyes watched her master.

"Beans." The old man strained the word through his teeth as if he had hated to say it.

"You want some beans to eat?"

"No. That's the trouble, boy. And now I know it for certain. All I been eatin' is beans, beans, beans. And now I'm to pay the price."

"I don't understand."

"Somehow they bloated my belly. It's the gas. Blowed me up like a balloon. My gut feels like it'll swell up with hot air and bust me to bits." Clenched hands held up his belly as he lay on one hip.

"Mr. Kirk, I'm going to examine you."

"Hell you are. Don't touch me nowhere."

"Sorry."

With a careful hand, I slowly undid the long row of buttons that covered his chest and abdomen, expecting any moment to have to dodge a punch from his gnarled fists. Sabbath Kirk had hands like hammers.

"Easy now, Mr. Kirk."

In contrast to the whiteness of his flat, hairless chest, his belly was pink and bloated. Beneath my fingers, the flesh was on fire. Gently, I poked his left side with little reaction. But when I touched his right side, his entire body convulsed.

He screamed.

22

"It's your appendix."

The old man grunted. "You think you know more 'n I give you credit for. But you ain't in the medical business."

"I told you that my grandfather is a doctor, and I bone through his books. Plus, I've taken a course in advanced first aid. One of the dangers they warn you about is the threat of rupturing an appendix."

"Well, I ain't got no rupture."

"Mr. Kirk, I want you to talk honestly to me, as truthful as a Vermont man ought."

"Shoot."

"We've all had stomachaches. But have you ever felt pain like this before?"

"Not never this bad. My old gut's been heated up and hurted for a few days, but each hour this turns worse. Hotter and sharper. Like somebody stickered me under the belt with a hog hook."

I had to think. Mr. Kirk was right about the beans,

as the many platefuls I had eaten had excited my own bowels several times a day. So, I concluded, beans are a laxative. If they behave like a laxative, then they are just that. The old man had eaten a limited diet of exactly what he should have avoided.

"How bad is it, Mr. Kirk?"

"I can't swallow the pain." He was gripping his belly again, his knees up against his chest. "This morning I took a couple of swigs of mineral oil. It'll loosen me up so's I can creep out back to the throne and set myself free."

"You what?"

Looking, I saw the bottle of mineral oil near the head of his cot. I hated believing what he had just told me. As if the beans were not enough, the old codger had dosed himself with mineral oil. A strong laxative. He had done the worst possible thing.

"You—gotta help me, boy." His voice was breaking; the words that came out were fragmented as if each was being pounded by pain. "I ain't never—*never* felt it like this. Same pain, in the same old spot. But it ain't never—stuck me so dreadful sharp."

"How close is the nearest doctor?"

"A day away."

"Where?"

"Over to—Dresden."

"I'll go and bring him, if I have to run every step."

"No—don't go, boy."

"We can't wait, Mr. Kirk. You said you were feeling as if your insides were going to explode. Well,

you're right. That's it. Maybe your appendix is going
to pop."

"Yeah."

"Tell me exactly what you feel."

"Like—I'm a blowed up—steam boiler."

"How far is Dresden in miles?"

"Don't know. Never did care—to learn. But it
don't matter, boy. When you get back, I'll be—
dead."

He screamed again. "Please, boy—you gotta *do*."

Wetting a rag, I bathed the sweat from his face.
His eyes were shut tight, and his chin trembled beneath its scanty white whiskers.

"Listen—to me—boy."

"I'm right here. And I won't leave you. Honest, I
won't."

He grabbed my hand with the strength of a lobster
claw. "I know. Listen. What's in me, son—it's gotta
come out—and you best do it now."

"Do what?"

"Take it out of my belly. Now—*now!*"

"I'm no doctor. I can't—"

"You *can*. Collin, I know you'll do her—whatever
she be that needs did. I trust you, boy." Holding both
of my hands in his, he squeezed until I was afraid all
my knuckles would split.

"I know ya, boy—in a couple three days, I now
knowed you proper. What's in ya's good. But—what's
in me is bad—and it best get took out, on account I
can't—I can't no longer abide it."

"You want me to—"

The old man looked into my eyes, nodding his rigid head at me. "Whatever it be, fetch it clean out of me —and sudden. Right now."

I swallowed. "Do you have any whiskey? Brandy? Anything like that?"

He pointed.

Fetching the bottle, I yanked out the cork and smelled. "This is potent booze. What is it?"

"Apple—brandy."

"Here, drink some of it."

He drank several healthy swallows.

"How strong is it?" I asked.

"She'll kick."

I didn't know what that meant. All I did was hold the small bottle as the old man fired his throat, his skinny neck bobbing down the tart-smelling brandy.

"Finish it. Drink every drop if you can."

I couldn't find the soap, and I dropped a tin can on the floor in panic. Steady, I warned myself. Stay cool and calm. Don't blow this one, Pepper.

Finding soap at last and rolling up my shirt-sleeves, I lathered myself from fingertips to elbows. My mind whirled. Who do I think I am? And what in hell am I doing? Why me? My body shook. Because I'm Collin Pepper, and I'm the only one here, that's why. And, by damn, I can take apart the whole doggone world if it can help save . . .

Tool barked.

"Please, old girl," I said.

Luckily there was hot water in the kettle that the old man had started preparing as I had arrived home. Like an idiot, I rinsed my hands under the tilted kettle spout and scalded my fingers almost raw.

God, can I do it? There wasn't time to pray. This whole operation was going to be a prayer, and I'd be begging heaven for one hell of a bundle. Dashing outside, I came back with a stack of clean meat-cloths. Clean? Should I boil them? What should I do next? Find surgical tools.

Sabbath Kirk groaned. "Hurry."

Still seeing brandy left in the bottle, I said, "Drink it up."

"I—can't."

"Drink it, you stubborn old man. Swallow it all or I won't . . ." I couldn't finish my thought.

In a cupboard, I found a treasure, a bottle of carbolic acid, which I poured into a pot and carefully diluted with hot water. Then I scalded and sterilized the hunting knife. It was sharp and clean. Turning over all Mr. Kirk's precious old coffee cans, I found enough junk to repair the *Queen Elizabeth* ocean liner or a Boeing jet. Sabbath Kirk was a saver, a hoarder of spare hardware consisting of everything ever lost or manufactured. Clips to clothespins.

Wondering how many scalpels surgeons used, I decided that one knife was all my hands could hold, ergo employ.

God, can I save him? I asked myself over and over as I thought what to do next.

Grabbing a plastic sweater bag out of one of my suitcases, I ran outside and filled it with snow. Then carefully I placed it over his abdomen, hoping the cold would locally freeze his body so he'd be numb. Besides booze, snow was the only available anesthetic.

Looking at my impressive display of surgical instruments spread out on a meat rag, I counted one hunting knife, tweezers, five clips of assorted sizes, a needle, half a spool of boiled thread, plus a handful of clothespins, for which I fervently thanked the Lord. All this and five old spoons. Everything doused in the carbolic acid.

You're bright, Collin. Teachers always told me that. Smart but lazy. You could become anything you want to be, Collin. They'd told me that, too. I was a goof-off, a playboy, a problem kid who'd been given psychiatric analysis instead of a swift kick in the butt.

Oh, God, I'm scared. Please, if You're up in Heaven, hang with me on this one, and I won't ask You for another damn thing. You gave me the guts to do it and the brains, I hope, to do it. So here goes. I carried my stuff to an overturned box by the cot and looked down at Mr. Kirk. "Here," I told him, jamming a pine twig between his yellow teeth. "Bite it and pray."

Not wanting to wait for more morning light, I lit every candle stub I could find. All seven. Then I sat down astride his thighs, starting to cry, feeling the fright run in rivulets down my face. I brushed them away with the back of my hand.

"Come on, candy-ass," I said aloud. "Do it."

Quickly I removed the bag of melted snow, washed my hands and his swollen belly with soap and hot water, and gently patted him dry. I picked up the hunting knife.

Tool whined, but lay still.

As I made the first bloody cut into his flesh, I felt the old man's pain stab up through the knife handle, into my hand, and all the way into my heart.

23

I prayed he was drunk.

The top of my incision began halfway between his right hipbone and his navel. Five inches long, it slanted downward from slightly below his waist toward his crotch.

He was bleeding. Prepared for this, I dabbed away the blood, spreading the incision open with two spoons. Bending them, I used the spoons to hold his belly open. Beneath the fleshy tissue, I came to another covering that, at first, puzzled me. It was an inner wall, a thin and filmy layer of grayish-white that looked like wet, shiny plastic.

Remembering my grandfather's book on abdominal surgery, I knew this inner layer was often called an apron. One picture in that book was now clear in my mind.

I could hear Grandfather's voice. "Surgery is never the first answer, lad. It is only the final resort."

Mr. Kirk bled. I sopped up his blood from each rim

of the incision. Was I making a mistake? Did I cut instead of think?

Using two more spoons, I spread the incision wider. And my next step became clearer. The filmy apron tightened against his insides.

Bull's-eye! There it was, his appendix beneath the film. Not that I could see it. But I knew its exact location. I felt it, where I knew it would be, attached to where his smaller bowel fed into the larger. Somehow I could see what I could not see.

Pressing with my fingers, I felt his appendix. It was about as long as my middle finger, yet it did not feel swollen. Had it been swollen earlier and ruptured?

You've got to remember all you've read, Collin, I told myself as I felt again, finding no limpness and yet no bloated condition that threatened a rupture. No, I won't use the knife here. There's no need. But there is pain. Why? The old man said that something inside him had to come out.

Mr. Kirk's head rolled from side to side, and muffled pain strained from him with every breath. I should have roped his wrists. His fingers clawed downward as though wanting to throttle my hands.

"It's not your appendix," I told him, trying also to tell myself that I was guessing right.

But, for some reason, I knew my work had only begun. There was more to do. His belly was too bloated, too sore, to have been inflated by what I concluded was a near-normal appendix.

Reaching for a candle, I held the flickering light as

close as possible without burning him. With my right hand, I carefully probed inside the incision with the tip of one finger. I found something. Not being able to see it, I felt it all. Big as a baseball, it was round, rubbery, not terribly hard.

A tumor? It was punching upward, as if trying to penetrate the soft apron.

After exploring it thoroughly, I rejected the tumor idea. Remembering what I had read, I concluded a tumor would have felt more firm. This, to the contrary, was some giant sac of pus. An abscess. How the devil would I sever the stem of an object I could neither see nor reach?

My finger nudged it again, causing the old man's legs to kick upward at me, even though I had been careful to sit on his knees and thighs.

"What do I do now?" I asked aloud. I can't close him up again and leave this monster inside him. Should I make a second incision, a deeper one? No, I thought, blotting away the persistent blood that kept gushing in and around the spoons. No, I won't cut him any more.

My hands were shaking. Looking down at my bloody fingers, I snatched at a rag to clean them. The rag reddened. Scrubbing my palms, I remembered my blisters, earned by the ax and saw on the day we cut and hauled our firewood.

Was that yesterday? Day before? Or a hundred years ago? The blisters had quickly healed. The old man had popped them so the fluid would drain out.

No, he had not cut the blisters out of my palms. Only punctured them.

I forced myself to think clearly—and to remember my grandfather's books. What's an abscess? Isn't it just some fancy medical term for a blister or a pimple? Maybe I won't have to hack it out. I've probably done enough damage in here.

A noise startled me! One of the spoons slipped, popping out, hitting the iron stove, then landing on the plank floor with a pathetic clank—as if to tell me it wanted no further role in my butchery of its owner.

I was thankful that Mr. Kirk had made me gut the deer. Because now I wasn't sick or throwing up. Scared out of my skull maybe, but at least I'd come this far.

Calmly I told myself that I had not, in panic, removed the wrong item. His appendix was not my target. I felt relieved that I had listened whenever Grandfather told me about performing surgery.

Whatever I do now, I decided, I had best guess right and do it. Okay, I conclude that an abscess is a blister that I don't attempt to remove. I drain it.

Gripping the old man's body, I slowly rolled him over onto his left hip. He now faced the wall, and the light was worse, but I didn't need to see anything for the moment. It was all feel. After replacing the slipped-out spoon with a clean one, I picked up the tweezers and felt my careful way to the abscess.

The old man let out a holler, and his free hand fought my face, slapping at me as I tortured him.

"Hang on," I told him.

As I jabbed the sharp ends of the tweezers through the apron and into what I prayed was the abscess ball, I felt my fingertips suddenly drown in a hot torrent of fluid. Was it pus? I held the tweezers in place a few moments to keep the punctures aligned. Then, removing the tweezers, I saw that they and my hand were coated with a putrid substance, a cloudy yellow that reeked with infection.

Poking one finger through the tiny hole in the apron, I felt for the abscess. It was gone. Only the soppy sac remained, limp and lifeless, deflated in its death.

Mr. Kirk swore into the stick he was gnawing on, while I did my best to thoroughly absorb the remaining pus. Most of it had erupted out of him.

Rolling the old man back to belly up, I dabbed a few cautious drops of the dilute carbolic acid through the hole and onto the punctured sac, to reduce the chance of any infection. He kicked and bucked beneath me.

I thought about using the carbolic acid on his main incision and decided against it. Even diluted, it might cauterize the tissue enough to keep it from healing properly. So I'd just do the rest with my boiled thread.

I couldn't find my needle. Everything around me seemed to be wet with blood or caked with it dry. Finally, I located the needle, threaded it, and meticulously began to remove my spoons. The wound closed.

I needled in a row of stitches. Some were long and others short.

"What a mess," I said.

Tying and trimming the last stitch, I realized that this was the first sewing job I'd ever performed in my entire life. Wow! If Mom could only see this—and Luroleen, too. No, on second thought, I guess I wouldn't want them here. They'd both faint. Not because of what they would see, but because Collin Pepper was the kid who did it.

Was Mr. Kirk breathing?

With my ear to his naked chest, I listened for his heart. Yes, it was beating. He was alive. Only not moving, and no doubt passed out from the pain. Pressing his chest with my hands, I figured I was helping him to breathe. Maybe the old man was numb from a combination of blood loss, pain, and brandy.

I hoped for the last. Touching his stubbled face, I thought, What a tough old bird. A wounded eagle. There sure was one hell of a layer of winter bark on Sabbath Kirk. My part had been the easy part. All I had done was cut, stab, and sew. But he had ridden his cot and eaten his agony.

It was a dumb thing to say out loud, but I didn't care. I just looked at him and said it: "Get well soon."

After washing his laced-up belly, I dried him with my last clean rag, buttoned his underwear, and fell down on the floor. Those worn boards suddenly became the most beautiful and comfortable bed in the world.

My hand stretched over to touch the heat of his wrist so I could rest, feeling his pulse. Its throb was slow, weak, but at least his heart was pumping. Thank God.

Tool crawled close to me.

24

It was dark.

My eyes opened, and I wondered who I was, where I was, and why my body had become so wooden. I smelled a dog near my face.

"Winnie?"

A dog's strong breath exhaled into my nose, as a rough tongue licked my cheek. I flinched, trying to move, feeling little more than the hardness beneath me and inside me.

"I'm so cold."

Please, somebody, I thought, bring me a blanket. And a pillow. Stuff it under my head. Yes, and while you're at it, I'm so thirsty I could spit cotton. I want water.

"Mom?"

I heard someone moan. Is there somebody here in my room?

"Who is it?"

Everything was dark confusion. Plus my bed felt so

hard. They put boards under my sheets. And it's so cold here. Turn up the heat, Mom.

Another moan.

"Hey," I said through my iron face, "who's there?"

"Boy?"

The voice—it came from nearby, only a foot or so away, it seemed. Blinking, I tried lifting my head so I could learn what had happened to me.

Where's my coat? I wondered. I've got to put my coat on. I'm freezing.

Crawling over a dog, I moved on hands and knees, bumping my head on something hard. A sink cabinet. Clutching its edges, I pulled my body upward to look out a small window. Snow. All white out there.

Suddenly I remembered. I'm not home! This is the shack up in Vermont where I'm living with the old man.

Feeling water in a bucket, I splashed my face with it, hoping the shock would jolt some awareness into my brain. It did. As I drank deeply from the dipper, the madness of remembering it all punched me awake.

The old man? Squinting, I could see him on his cot. Was he asleep or dead? Tripping over Tool, who yelped at me, I halfway fell into the foot of the cot. I listened and finally heard the raw breathing of old lungs.

"Are you alive?"

"Collin—you . . ."

Hearing him made me smile. And breathe.

"Mr. Kirk?"

"My belly's near to—killing."

"It's out." Memory flooded my mind, and I saw Loomis Broom, the butchered deer, the gun, the two hens, the open bloody abdomen of the old man. "I took it out, Mr. Kirk. Honest."

"Night—dark . . ."

"It's okay," I told him. "Don't be afraid. I did it. The pain you feel is because of what I had to do."

I pulled up his blanket and tucked it around him. Trying to see his face more clearly, I moved down closer, smelling the stale stench of used brandy. My hand found his forehead. It was still hot, but cooler than the furnace it had been earlier.

"Are you okay, Mr. Kirk? You're not cold or anything, are you?"

"I'm—living."

His voice was puny, almost childlike, as though some old doll was lying under the blanket and had learned to whisper. I held his hand and felt his hard fingers try to press mine. He didn't seem to have an ounce of power.

I heard a whine.

"Tool?"

She came at my call and stood and rested her chin on the edge of the cot, beside me and as close as she could get to the old man. Her tail thumped again and again, drumming the woodbox. I liked the noise her tail made. If Tool was happy, then so was I.

"He's okay," I told her.

Stroking her satiny head made me stronger. Thirsty,

hungry, cold—yet I felt the urgings of life: Tool's life, mine, and the life of this brave old man.

My mind filled. Wow! I can't believe it all. The kid came through, and I'm really getting a rush out of it. Whatever job has to be done now, I'll handle it. Lay it on me, world. It's my turn.

I never thought it would be a cinch to pluck and clean two frozen chickens in the dark. I was probably making one awful mess, but at least I couldn't see it. Compared to surgery, this little chore was a snap. I filled the cooking pot with water, stirred up the fire, and set the water to boiling. Hacking the hens apart, I dumped them into the pot, adding the old dusty potatoes I'd found in one of the coffee cans. Laughing in the darkness, I even added a dozen heaping handfuls of beans. Whichever resulted, chicken stew or chicken soup, I didn't much care.

Right now, I would've earnestly sold my soul for one cool glass of milk. Or a creamy bite of chocolate ice cream. But no use in dreaming.

"Hope you like chicken, Tool."

Later, as it turned out, she did. I slid one of the griddles off the surface of the Acme American so I could see enough to ladle out supper, feed Tool, and then spoon some of my gourmet cooking into Mr. Kirk.

He ate. Only about six or seven spoons of chicken stew went into him, but he swallowed every one. Looking at me, he spoke just a word.

"Beans."

I felt a grin crack my face. "Yeah, I know. I'm a rotten chef. But I'm one hell of a doctor."

Sabbath Kirk nodded. "You—you saved . . ."

"Hey. Don't talk. You're not the honcho around here anymore. I just took over. Maybe if you get stronger and help me whack a few chores, I'll slip you a buck a month."

As I fed myself a drumstick, the old man pointed at the bowl I was holding. His face looked puzzled.

"Chicken?"

"Right. But don't ask. It's kind of a long story, and I'd hate to bore you with all the lurid details." I figured it was best not to tell him right now about my little trip to recover our meat, and how I'd ripped off Loomis Broom.

I kept eating. Even though I couldn't taste any potato, the chicken stew was one zinger of a meal. I had been really careful with the chicken bones, doubly so in the portion I'd dished out to the old man. And to Tool.

There were bones in my share, but I couldn't have cared less. The chicken was a bit on the tough side. But I hadn't honestly expected old Loomis to have raised anything very tender. Vermont was no delicate place.

Loomis had probably already eaten all the deer. Raw. I hoped the score was settled. World peace would certainly be enhanced by an armistice to end the famous feud between Broom and Pepper.

"Tool," I said, "I'm almost happy."

Walking to the door of the cabin, she looked at me with her brown eyes. I let her out. The world outside was white and still. A pure night. So this was April. Maybe we'd see a genuine spring by the Fourth of July.

How long had I been here? I was remarking to myself that I didn't know what day, or night, it was. Or what time. Yet it didn't seem to matter. I knew what was at the top of the list.

Sabbath Kirk mattered one heck of a lot.

I ate more of my chicken stew, more beans, until my fork was finally rewarded with half a boiled potato for dessert. Chewing it slowly, I made it last a long time.

The old man stirred and muttered.

After feeling his belly, I figured that he needed some attention. I went outside, filled the sweater bag with fresh snow, and applied it as gently as possible over his incision. The ice pack might do double duty: help to reduce the swelling and reduce his fever. Plus, if we were lucky, numb away part of his pain. The brandy was gone. So I could merely use snow on his belly.

He wasn't complaining. Yet nobody can have his gut carved up and concentrate on too much else. Every breath he sucked in must have felt like fire.

"Hang in there, Mr. Kirk."

The strong smell of abscess still stayed with him. I would have to do something about fresh clothes and a cleaner bed. But not now. I didn't want to move him and risk tearing open his stitches. He'd have an ugly scar on his belly. Like a misplaced zipper.

After cleaning up the dishes and picking up my litter of hen feathers, I added water to the rest of the stew, deciding to let it simmer and become more tender. The slow cooking would also prevent its collecting any bacteria, seeing as there was no refrigerator.

Ha! Glancing out the sink window, I knew the joke was on me. No refrigerator? We were living in one. Vermont was its own icebox. The stars sparkled through the high branches. I noticed one star in particular, hanging like a distant medal on the blue tunic of midnight.

"Sleep tight," I told Mr. Kirk.

I lay down and slept.

25

Day came, and another night.

As to time or date, I was hopelessly lost. Again and again, I brought in snow and ice-packed the old man's belly. His fever had become even more stubborn than his nature.

His bed fouled. So, item by item, I removed his bedclothes and his underwear, keeping him warm with blankets and some of my clothes and stove heat, yet cooling his gut with snow. It was lucky that we had soap and water and a fire to help my washing. Every hunk of cloth that I could grab got scrubbed with soap and lake sand, then dried behind the Acme American.

I shaved him every day. Maybe if he began to feel and look healthy, he'd heal.

More snow fell, and we were down to a handful of peanuts and our last few cups of white beans. The chicken stew had been eaten and the pot scoured. Tool and I gobbled up a can of solid bacon grease. I fought to keep from gagging, and I kept it down. I shot a few gray squirrels with the Purdey, and we ate squirrel and beans.

Mr. Kirk ate very little. Almost nothing. So I made him drink water, hoping he wouldn't urinate in his cot. He didn't. The fever turned all the water into a steamy film that seemed to cling to his skin, regardless of how frequently I'd try to bathe him cool.

My own belly was now swollen, with emptiness. And during one mad and starving moment, I looked at the dog. Could I eat Tool?

Taking the double-bitted ax, I hacked into the frozen ground to dig up tree roots until my fingertips were numb and bleeding. I boiled them to eat. Boiled roots are stringy, tough, and bitter. Tool was hunger thin, still too weak to hunt for herself or for us. Yet she turned up her nose at boiled roots.

Outside there was no game. Not even a rat. The Purdey hung uselessly on its two pegs. I made sure it was loaded and ready to kill anything that moved. Even a sparrow.

A thaw came. Icicles dripped steadily from the rim of our roof. Yet outside the snow was still deep enough to defy walking. Because our fuel supply had dwindled, I cut and split more wood. No blisters formed, except for one bubble that I looked at with contempt. It broke, and I peeled off the wet skin and ate it.

Days dawned, and nights came. On and off. Sleeping often, in short naps on my bedroll, I dreamed of

Luroleen Bunkum back home in our spacious and spotless kitchen. I even smelled all the food: turkey, ham, roast beef, popovers with melting butter inside their steam, pies and cakes and puddings.

Awake, I tried to remember the beauty of the War Head, to at least replenish my spirit.

The worst came, as I feared it might.

I had seen his tracks outside, to the north of our cabin, and knew that he had come to spy on us. Or steal whatever we had. He always came at night.

Loading the Purdey, I waited for him in the dark, knowing that he would probably come again. If he did, I'd shoot.

He came.

"Bandit?"

The raccoon crept closer, his paws buried with each step into the wet snow.

"Come on, and you'll get a peanut," I urged.

Liar! Mr. Kirk's peanuts had been devoured, as had every scrap of food. I couldn't swallow another root.

Bandit was less than a hundred feet away, a dark furry hunk of curiosity. I wondered if he, too, was hurting to eat. Animals also probably starved in winter. But as I slowly raised the loaded Purdey, I knew that Bandit's fate would not be hunger.

The gun weighed a ton. It felt heavier and harder than I could remember since the last time I had sighted it, to kill a gray squirrel. My arms trembled, waiting for the raccoon to conquer his instinct of danger.

He didn't know. All he probably sensed was that this was the strange-smelling place where a larger animal tossed him a nightly peanut. He was unaware of the Purdey—because he had come before, to trust, to taste an unfamiliar but delicious morsel, a peanut from an old man.

"That's it, Bandit. Keep coming."

I would not hate myself. Even though I was going to slaughter the raccoon who, in a wild way, had become a friendly visitor.

Bandit came closer.

"Come on."

The Purdey shook in my hands. Pressing the stock to my cheek, I took one final look along the barrel at Bandit, then pulled the trigger, hearing the blast, choking on the stink of charcoal and saltpeter and regret.

Bandit kicked in the wet snow.

I cleaned the raccoon, boiled it until the meat fell off the bones, and we ate it. As it cooked, Tool was almost mad for her food. Insane though it was, I divided the meat into thirds—for Tool, the old man, and me.

When the meat was gone, we drank the broth in the pot. Tool lapped up her share.

"Collin—"

Mr. Kirk was trying to sit up. He had tried before several times, but the fever and agony had held him down. With my arm behind his shoulders, I boosted him up, then helped him swing his skinny legs off the cot and onto the floor.

"I want—"

"Yes?"

"Want to sit—my rocker."

"You bet. Hang on tight."

Somehow I moved him, one unsteady step at a time, across the cabin floorboards to his rocking chair. His weight, little as it was, was all I could support. No sooner had he sat in his rocker than my knees buckled. I sank to his feet.

"Boy?"

"I'm okay."

"You—you're weak."

"No," I tried telling him. "Not me."

"I sure do thank you—Collin."

My head rested on the floor. I was just too tired to sit up or stand. What was I going to feed Mr. Kirk for supper? Or was suppertime over? What time was it? Which day? I felt my eyes close.

"We're alive," the old man said huskily.

Tool joined us, lying close to me on the floor and resting one of her paws over my hand.

Fight, I ordered myself. Don't quit now. Think of something funny. Lip off a wise remark as you used to do. I forced my eyes open.

"I got some good news, Mr. Kirk."

"What is it?"

I smiled. "We're out of beans."

The rockers rolled on the rough boards to tell me

that the old man was laughing. Then I heard his laughter and saw his thin hand lift up to slap a sharp knee.

"Boy—that's a gooder."

"Are we licked?"

He chuckled again. "Us? I hope to Harry we ain't."

"I'm not so sure."

"You an' me—we're a thorny two."

"I hope so."

"Collin—I never had me no grandson." He stopped to rest his words. "But I sure got me you."

My eyes clenched shut. Also my fists. The old man didn't have much, and yet he had it all. Right then, I knew he had me for a friend, right down to the last bean and the last boiled root.

I forced myself to think and not sleep. Do I have the strength to get up off this floor, take the Purdey, and hunt? Sure I do. Then why am I shaking? Come on, loser. Collect your guts together. But it's so cold outside, and lonely. This mountain is the end of the end.

"Your grandpa—"

"What about him?" I asked.

"The one you say is a doc."

"That's right."

"I bet he's right proud of you."

Everything that Mr. Kirk was saying was hurting. Cutting into me.

"And," the old man said, "so's your dad."

"No, nobody's proud of me. I'm the family misfit.

That's why Dad brought me here. For you to doctor me up."

Mr. Kirk laughed softly. "Looks to me like they got it all backwards. I'm getting well, boy. Feel like I could lick old Loomis."

What I needed right then was a spur. Maybe we both did. A real kicker. So now was the time to tell him the truth.

"Remember the chicken stew?"

"Yup."

"I stole it."

"You what?"

"Somebody took our deer."

"Figured so. Never smelled it cook."

"Well, you're right. That guy Loomis Broom helped himself to it. Dragged it all the way to his place. So I loaded the Purdey and took out after him."

"No."

"Yes. I tracked him to his family's shack and stole two of their hens. And I let the rest of their chickens run loose."

Looking up at Mr. Kirk, I saw his wide smile and glistening eyes. His entire body was shaking, and his face appeared as though it would crack open. He slapped his knee again. But then his grin froze, and he grabbed his belly.

"Damn it, boy."

I sat up. "What's wrong?"

"The fun's about to pop my thread."

26

"Collin, do us a turn."

Mr. Kirk was lying on his cot, twisting his face toward me, speaking softly. I was busy poking wood into the Acme American.

"Sure," I said.

"Bundle your coat on, and go north to the lake."

"What for?"

"Hear me out."

His voice had a sharpness to it just then, and I welcomed the sound. He was mending.

"Turn east from the lake and follow a crick bed down a holler. Abide it and don't wander wild. Hear?"

"I hear."

"You'll downhill it all the way to a footbridge. Near to three mile. Right there you leave the crick lonesome and walk south. Follow the path and you'll arrive smart."

"What's there?"

"You'll hit a settle of six, maybe seven, shacks. The smallest is where you're to go knock. It's got a horseshoe over the door."

"Okay."

"Miss Biddy'll answer."

"Who's she?"

"Well, she's sort of distant kin to me. By marriage. Tell her who you be and why you come."

"For food, I hope."

Mr. Kirk nodded. "Ask how her lumbago is, and she'll brew ya some hot tea. If'n she slips a spike to it that tastes hotter than a hymnbook, pretend you don't take no notice."

"Right."

"Miss Biddy will load you up proper. No cans. They cost too dear a price. Ask her to put it all on the cuff so's I can settle up with her later."

"What'll I bring back?"

"Yourself, if'n you're lucky. I want flour, sugar, salt pork, coffee, bacon, potatoes—my usual. Miss Biddy knows."

I winked at him. "And beans?"

The old man chuckled. "Yes, by dandy! I got raised on 'em, so I might to well *die* on 'em, too."

"Anything else?" I asked him.

Mr. Kirk sat up on one elbow, scratching the inside of his underwear. "Soap. And a quarter wheel of rat cheese. You reckon you got the gumption to tote it all back?"

"I sure can."

"Collin, one more thing. Miss Biddy's got a cow, so ask her to please afford you as much milk as you can drink down. And add it to my cuff."

I shot him a grin.

"Now git. And don't let her overcharge you. When she totals it up, make sure she sees you're watching her pencil."

"Mr. Kirk, I hope that's all the instructions. Because I won't be able to remember it all." As I spoke, I was writing out his grocery list on a scrap of brown paper.

"One more thing, boy. Take the Purdey."

I took it. There was no sense in arguing with him about the gun. The old man didn't know how weak I had become. My knees were pudding. And the Purdey would just be needless weight, especially when I'd be loaded up like a pack mule, returning uphill to our shack. The gun would be of little or no use. So when I reached the lake and found the near-dry creek bed, I stashed the Purdey in a spruce crotch, covering it with a broken bough.

Following the creek was a piece of cake.

I turned south on the path at the footbridge and almost bumped into the shacks. I knocked at the smallest one. The door opened to reveal a large woman wearing a bright shirt of red wool, a railroad engineer's cap, and bib overalls. I figured her age was between thirty and forty.

She frowned. "Yeah?"

"Hello, I'm Collin Pepper."

"Maybe you be, and maybe you ain't."

"Are you Miss Biddy?"

"Well, I ain't exactly Little Bo Peep or Typhoid Mary. What in the Sam Hill do *you* want?"

"Uh—how's your lumbago?"

Miss Biddy rubbed an ample hip. "Hurts worse 'n Hades and burns like sin. Not that it's any of your business. You ain't from around here. Say, I ain't gonna stand with my door open so's I can heat the whole dang outdoors. Come inside."

I came in. Behind me, Miss Biddy slammed the door as I looked around the one room. The four walls were lined with shelves stacked with provisions. I spotted several items on Mr. Kirk's list. There were no curtains, no rugs, and no chairs. The cabin seemed designed to hold three large objects and only those: one giant stove, an enormous double bed, and Miss Biddy herself.

"Well?" she snorted.

Before I could answer her question, my nose began to ask one of its own. Atop the big stove, a black kettle was steaming with stew. My hunger hit me so hard that I was speechless. Before thinking, I took a step toward the stove. A big hand grabbed my skinny shoulder and spun me around.

"Look here, *you* . . ."

"My name's Collin Pepper."

"So ya say. Whatcha want?"

"Mr. Kirk sent me." After I said it, my head turned to look at the stove again. And its stew. The stew gave off a magnetic smell that made my mouth pop open.

"You mean old Wishbone sent ya here?"

I nodded. It was warm in her cabin, and my legs felt unsteady. But there was no chair to sit in. Inside my coat, I began to perspire.

"You sick?"

"No. I guess I'm just—"

"Stick out your tongue."

"Mr. Kirk told me to come and—"

"Boy, I told you to stick your tongue out, and I ain't just talkin' to the rafters. Stick it out."

I stuck out my tongue.

Tilting her head for a close view, Miss Biddy squinted at me, looking into each of my eyes. Her big hand shot up and rested on my brow.

"You feverish?"

"No, I don't think so."

"Well, you look puny to me. How long's it been since you ate a full meal?"

For an answer, I looked at her stove once again. "To tell you the truth, I don't honestly remember. I'm sorry. I didn't mean to barge in and—"

"Hush up and sit down."

I slumped down on the big bed that was covered by a faded quilt.

Miss Biddy's boots reached the stove in about one step. Opening the warming oven above the stove, she pulled out a large tin plate, which clattered as it met the black griddle below. A generous spoon dived into the stew and reappeared laden with brown meat, onions, potatoes, carrots, and gravy.

She handed me the steamy meal along with a fork that had a broken tine. "Eat up."

I ate it all in less than a minute.

"Don't he feed you up yonder?"

With my mouth working on the last bite, I said, "Mr. Kirk's been sick. I'm sort of his doctor. He's been real bad, and I've been looking after him."

"Somebody best look to *you*. Want more?"

"Yes! Please."

She spooned out another heap of stew. "Tell old Wishbone that I'm sorry he's off his feed. He's a good neighbor. Minds his business, which is more 'n I can say for some others."

I ate, pausing only to tell her, "Mr. Kirk says he'll pay for what I take."

"Fine. His word's always good."

"Do you have a cow?"

"Ha! I wager you want to wash down all that stew with a swaller of milk."

"Please."

Lifting a latch, Miss Biddy yanked an earthenware jug into the cabin, tilted it, and filled a dipper. In my mouth and throat, the milk was burning cold, but fresh and sweet. I couldn't stop drinking until the dipper was overhead, and my eyes could count its speckles.

"Well," asked Miss Biddy, "do I got a cow or ain't I?"

"You sure do. Thanks."

"Forget it. Her name's Buttercup. I git offers all the time to sell her. But I raised her up from a calf. Before I'd sell Buttercup, I'd sell my soul to Satan."

"It's really good."

"Want more?"

The dipper filled and emptied again, and I smiled. "Thanks, Miss Biddy. Thank you a whole lot."

"Aw, don't mention it. A pretty gal like me don't get no gent to knock on her door much cuter 'n you. How old be ya?"

"Fifteen."

Miss Biddy winked at me. "That's old enough for any sport that don't need no license."

The way she said it made us both laugh—though I wasn't so sure it was entirely a joke.

She nodded toward the bed. "Why don't you lie down and rest, sonny, while I get together your stuff."

"I've got a list of the supplies Mr. Kirk wants."

"Don't waste your breath. I'll stuff a sack with what he's to get. I know what that old coot wants better 'n *he* does."

Falling over on her big playground of a bed, I closed my eyes. In my stomach, the stew and milk would just have to fight it out. I'd eaten and drunk myself into a stupor.

I felt Miss Biddy loosen my coat, push a pillow under my head, and then pull off my boots.

She said, "Sweet baby lamb."

I slept.

27

"Hey!"

My eyes opened.

"I got your sack packed," said Miss Biddy. "Best you get yourself cranked up into a start before she gets dark."

"Okay." I sat up on the big bed.

"You sturdy enough to tote all this uphill?"

"Yes'm. I can do it."

Rubbing my eyes, I wanted to lie down again, sleep a year, wake up, eat stew and drink more of Buttercup's milk, and just live with Miss Biddy forever. Or at least until I grew to her size.

"You awake?"

"I guess so. And I'd really like to say thank you for the meal. Some time ago—I don't honestly know how long—Mr. Kirk and I sort of ran out of food. Days and days ago."

"Well, best you get cracking back. Before the darksome overtakes ya. And if you ever fetch yourself

down this way again, tarry around. You're cuter than
a coonhound pup. By the way, my name's Biddy Bidwell. And right now I ain't exactly wedded or bed-
ded."

I swallowed. Hurriedly I pulled on my boots, buttoned my jacket, grabbed the sack of provisions, and
said good-bye. But she blocked the door with her
body.

"Don't I get no kiss?"

Why not? I thought, and hugging her, I gave her a
kiss on the cheek. I don't imagine there was any more
of a rush in it for Miss Biddy than for me. It was sort
of the way, years ago when I was in elementary
school, that I'd embraced Luroleen Bunkum.

"Good-bye," I said, "and thanks again."

"So long, soldier."

As I trudged along the path toward the footbridge,
I knew it would be a long five miles. Much of it
uphill. The neck of the burlap sack was knotted and
slung over my shoulder. Already it was feeling heavier.
Thank goodness I hadn't lugged along the Purdey.

Vermont days end quickly. In only a few weeks I
had learned about this phenomenon. I figured it was
still April and cursed myself for not asking Biddy Bidwell what date or day it was. I didn't even know the
time. There was still snow all over, a world of silent
white, not a high-noon gold-and-silver snow, but a
crust of gray-blue shadows.

I could no longer see the sun.

"Ah," I said aloud, "here's the bridge."

I heard the trickle of creek water rushing beneath the twisted hunks of ice and snow. Sometimes, beneath the icy mounds, I could see gray boulders, lying in the water every few feet. A herd of hard, gray, sleeping sheep.

A dog barked. It wasn't Tool because, by now, I knew her bark as well as I knew Mr. Kirk's. Was it Loomis Broom's dog? Couldn't be. Not this far away from Broom Manor.

The bark came again. It was impossible for me to tell from where. A long way off. The sound of the dog hurried my pace. After almost trotting for a hundred yards, I stopped again to listen and to switch the supply sack over a fresh shoulder. The burlap had started to scratch the left side of my neck.

The dog bugled again, making me wish that I had brought Tool with me. It was a short series of yaps followed by one long howl. Then echoes, as though the yodel of the dog was answering itself.

Wolves? Easy now, Pepper, I told myself. You heard Mr. Kirk say there weren't any wolves in Vermont. Does he know? He knows. Mr. Kirk knows everything that's worth knowing and not much that isn't.

I started running again.

Okay, I thought, so there are no wolves. Yet I was trying to remember something Mr. Kirk had said about some other animals that were even more dangerous. I'd eaten too much and slept; my brain wasn't clicking. I wondered if it was true that your mind can't reason too sharply on a full stomach.

I heard another howl. And more. Closer.

What was the name of those animals? It wasn't fox or wolf. Jackal? Hyena? No, they're in Africa. Was it coyote?

Coydog! That was it. Amazing how I'd forgotten such an easy name. Maybe because I'd never heard the term before. But why was I worrying about remembering the name?

Run, you fool, I told myself.

The sack pounded my back with each stride, as my boots crashed upstream through the creek bed's jagged crust. Turning around, I squinted down the gully, seeing nothing but the black tree trunks that whiskered up through an endless face of snow.

I heard the coydogs again. Not just one, and more than two. How many? I couldn't seem to tell from which direction their howls came. Above me or below? Maybe I was crazy to run uphill. Maybe, if I was smart, I'd turn around and head back for that little family of shacks and get to Miss Biddy, who appeared as if she could lick half the world.

How far have I come? I wondered. Without answering my own question, I turned and continued to trot up the creek bed. I'd come at least a mile. Maybe more. Two miles? Three? How many more to where I'd left the Purdey?

I ran, much faster now—uphill, and into an ending

day, feeling as though I was only moving toward a trap of deepening darkness, hearing again Miss Biddy's warning: "Before the darksome overtakes ya."

My brain churned. Am I being chased by fear, darkness, or dogs? I mustn't panic. People do nutty things when their emotions take over. I don't know for sure about the coydogs. And can't say for certain they're after me.

The next sound convinced me of their position.

Now I knew. The yowling came from below me; I guessed about half a mile. Much closer than before. Looking over my shoulder, I gave downhill a quick glance, saw nothing, and ran like holy hell.

The Purdey. If I can only get to the shotgun, I thought, I can scare the devil out of those dogs. Maybe they aren't coys. That's it. Maybe they're just farm dogs or hunting dogs or a kind old family pooch who gets regularly fed out of a dish in the kitchen by a kid who calls him Rover or Rusty or Sport or . . .

God, it's getting dark.

It was as though a giant breath of wind had made a wish for nighttime, then blown out the day's one last candle. No moon. Only a charcoal snow of deepening gray and angry purples. Black trees in a garden of blackness. And me running. Hurting lungs above hurting legs. A dry mouth.

My throat retasted the stew and the milk.

There was a leafless bush growing from a snow-frosted flat rock between the narrows of the creek bed. Reaching it, I grabbed a dead branch; holding on, I leaned over and threw up everything. All of Miss Biddy's marvel of a meal. Onion, carrots, potatoes, milk, and meat. Up it all came, heave after heave, until all that stayed in me was its taste. One sour memory.

Again the dogs threatened, so again I ran. Uphill, gripping the neck of the burlap sack with both hands. Behind me, I heard the coydogs, no doubt smelling what I had thrown up. I kept running. Then I had to stop and look back.

Three black forms fought beside the bush. Growling, snarling, they battled for the remains of my retched-up stew.

With numb fingers, I tore open the knot in the neck of the burlap, pulling out what I could smell as bacon. It wasn't in strips the way supermarkets package it. It was just one greasy three-pound hunk. I set the sack down, using my hands and teeth to tear the bacon into smaller chunks, and scattered them into the snow.

My lungs burned.

My sack failed to weigh less; in fact, even without the bacon, it felt heavier. I ran on.

"Help me," I cried into the wind.

Behind me, as I ran, I heard the coys battle over the bacon. Not enough to feed three wild dogs. Big dogs. Uphill, they now knew, was meat. Stew, then bacon, and then a . . .

God, where's the Purdey?

I looked back. Two dogs were distant, still searching for more bacon. The third was a hundred feet behind me, trotting. I saw the black shape and the pair of yellow pinpoint eyes. He smelled food, and I smelled his hunger. And I heard him pant.

Twisting my body, I churned up the gully.

Pepper, you're not going to die a quitter, I told myself. But maybe you are going to die. Now I knew why Mr. Kirk had ordered me to take the Purdey. But I'd parked it. Where? It had to be up ahead, but how far?

How much farther can I run? I wondered. I can't breathe. I've got to stop. My heart's going to burst. My lungs are about to explode. Run. Run. Drop the dumb sack and run.

I dropped it. Just let it slide out of my freezing fingers and back over my shoulder, to meet the snow crust with one soft crunching whimper. A sound of defeat. I saw a hunk of cheese tumble out and roll into the water. Gone.

It made me mad enough to fight.

Falling to my knees, I stabbed my hands into the icy water. But I didn't feel its cold. Snatching up a pair of small rocks, I threw two at the closest dog. I could see all three now. The first rock missed. It just melted into darkness as if I had thrown nothing more than some silent insult.

But my second rock hit a dog. I heard one painful yelp. This was followed by howls from the other two pair farther back. All I could see were fuzzy black shapes—and eyes, eyes, eyes.

Grabbing one more rock in reserve, I clawed up the sack and ran. Something else fell out, but I was beyond caring.

The spruce crotch! I reached it. The Purdey was loaded. I grabbed it, gasped for air, and I waited for the coys to come. And they came. Trot, trot, trot—not a canter or a gallop. Just an easy gait that seemed to threaten how confident they were that they could run down any living thing and tear out its throat.

My thumb clicked off the safety, and I waited. Soon they were there, and all I saw, was the front bead of my gun barrel between the closest pair of yellow eyes. Thirty feet away. Now twenty-five. Twenty.

I tried to calm myself. Steady on, Pepper. Don't blow it. All you have is one shell. Like an idiot, you forgot to pack along extras. One shot, and three coys.

I leaned against the spruce tree, smelling the raw bacon on my hands, remembering the old man's warning about jerking the trigger. Softly I squeezed, squeezed, squeezed.

Wham! There was a sudden and exploded stink of powder, a smoking barrel, and two dogs. The third was dead. The two turned and bolted, howling. One of them surely had been slightly wounded. The other possibly was only in panic. Grabbing our food sack and holding the Purdey, I ran south toward our cabin.

Mr. Kirk was awake.

A lantern burned at the window over the sink, and I knew he'd struggled out of his cot to light it. For me. To help guide me home. Tool licked my hand as I slumped into the rocker, still panting.

"I see you made it back," said Mr. Kirk.

"No trouble at all."

"How's Miss Biddy?"

"Fine. She fed me. She's got a cow, as you said, and she gave me two dippers of milk."

The old man undid the sack, inspecting each item as he withdrew it. Biddy Bidwell's selections seemed to meet his approval. I saw him smell the fresh bar of soap. But then he scowled slightly, looking up at me and snorting through his nose in his displeased voice.

"You forgot bacon."

28

We ate. Mr. Kirk, Tool, and I finished most of the food I had brought home in two days. Except for the beans. Now all we had was a small white bag of sugar, another of salt, and one of flour. We wolfed down all the salt pork and all the apples, plus a cut of ham.

We ate no bacon and no cheese, nor did I bother to explain to the old man how neither had come back with me. I had ignored his advice and left the Purdey where it might have been lost forever, had the coy-dogs caught me. So I kept mum.

I was asleep on my bedroll when I heard the old man coughing. He was awake.

"Mr. Kirk?"

"Here I be."

He was rolling up and out of his cot. So I helped him climb into his clothes. Other than beans and coffee, there was no breakfast to feed him or to feed Tool. I wanted to cry, but damned if I would.

Mr. Kirk told me he wanted to sit in his rocker, so I helped him to it. He was growing stronger. The sparkle had returned to his eyes, and to see it made me feel more resolute than I thought I could be.

We had slept late. I fed him a combination late breakfast and lunch of hot beans. He ate very little. Almost nothing. Well, I wasn't going to force food into him. Or into Tool. Yet I made myself eat about thirty beans. It was all I could keep down.

Each time I looked at the old man and the dog, I wondered just what I was going to do next. Another trip to Miss Biddy Bidwell's? No, I'd never make it. My legs were too weak. Maybe, with luck, I might make the five miles to her shack, but I could never return as a pack mule. I sat on the cot, petting the dog, smiling at Mr. Kirk, and doing my best to look brave.

Tool suddenly barked. Ears up, she jumped to her feet, spine rigid and bristling, to growl at the door of the cabin.

"Steady now, girl," the old man said. And then to me, he added, "Somebody's out there. Go see."

Would it be Loomis Broom?

Knees unwilling, I got up off the cot and went for the Purdey. If the Brooms and their black dog were here to stir up trouble, they'd soon learn that Sabbath Kirk and Collin Pepper and Tool were not going to be bullied. Not even by all the Brooms in Vermont.

Before reaching the gun, I heard voices. Tool heard them, too, and snarled. Her nose advanced close to the crack of our closed door. I pitied the first intruder, man or dog, who planned to charge into our cabin.

There was a knock. Then, "Hello in there."

I knew the voice. Leaving the Purdey on its pegs, I grabbed Tool and gently pulled her away from the door. "Stay," I told her with a pat. She was quiet, but her ears remained erect.

Mr. Kirk said, "Who is it, boy?"

Opening the door, I heard Tool roar her rage, but I managed to block her charge with my body. The two people standing in the melting snow outside the door looked at me as I looked at them. A second later I was between them, hugging them as they hugged me and feeling their joy surge into me.

"Mom! Dad!"

Tool was growling, and I could hear the old man trying to contain her. I prayed that she'd know there was no danger to her master or to me. I was hers now, too.

"Collin—Collin."

The softness of Mom's voice and her sweet fragrance flooded me as the three of us hugged and kissed. Even though I felt too gritty to touch anybody, it didn't seem to interfere.

Dad was smiling. He had a good face, and as I looked at him over Mom's shoulder, I wondered how I could have hated him.

"Well," he barked, "invite us in."

Mom asked, "Are you all right?"

We all went inside. Greetings were exchanged, and

Dad introduced Mom to Mr. Kirk, who struggled to his feet by the rocker. Tool, in her wisdom, seemed to know that I belonged to the newcomers as much as to her, and also that the old man was not in jeopardy.

My parents had each brought a shopping bag and looked around, not knowing what to do next.

"Please," I said, my voice shaking to match my body, "have a seat." As they sat on the squeaking springs of the cot, Tool stood beside Mr. Kirk in the rocker, her brown eyes still searching for signs of alarm. I saw her nostrils sucking information.

"It's been over three weeks," Dad said.

"Has it?"

"Your mother and I quite frankly were wondering how the two of you"—he looked at Tool—"the *three* of you were getting along."

Sabbath Kirk nodded. "We'll do."

My mother looked so perfectly groomed, so much like Greenwich, and so very foreign to our shack. I saw her eyes inspecting the cabin interior, and then she leaned over to pick up something on the floor. That's my mom, I thought. Always wanting to tidy up.

In her hand was a bent spoon.

I looked at Mr. Kirk's belly, remembering the precise moment that the spoon my mother was now holding had held the old man's abdomen open and had popped loose. Mom, I thought, if I told you about our recent days, you might faint. So might I.

"Well," said Dad, with his hands on his knees, "how's it going?"

Shaking my head and smiling at my parents, I didn't know how I could ever begin the chore of reporting the past events. Even if I did tell them, they probably wouldn't believe it.

I stood by the Acme American, watching my parents sitting on Sabbath Kirk's cot as if they were two roses that had somehow blossomed in a junkyard. They were dressed in sports clothes, the kind of tweedy outfits they wore to outdoorsy events, like tailgate picnics at Yale football games.

I wanted to tell them about Sabbath Kirk and Tool, about the rabbit I'd killed and Loomis Broom. About the cleaning and tracking of the deer, the stolen chickens, and my stew. Not to mention the surgery. But I didn't know where to start. Not with the coydogs. The more I thought about it, the less I wanted to share any of it. Bragging it all out would only be kid stuff.

Mr. Kirk glanced at me and then faced my parents again. "Collie—he's took hold real solid."

Dad smiled. "That's very good to hear, Mr. Kirk."

The old man rocked his chair once. "*I* don't much favor the young whelp—but Tool accepts him some." He winked at me.

Mom and Dad looked at each other, then back to me, the dog, the old man in his rocking chair. For a moment, I felt the desire for all of us to introduce ourselves. It was like a game. We three were the athomers, while Mom and Dad were the visiting team—strangers.

"Well now," Dad began again, "tell us what you gentlemen have been up to. Having fun?"

Mom added, "You look thin."

I prayed that I wouldn't howl with laughter. I imagined saying, "Mother, may I present Mr. Loomis Broom? Fine family. Lots of background. Until recently, lots of hens." Unable to hold it all back, my face grinned at Mom, and she echoed a somewhat hesitant, yet motherly, smile at me. I was one lucky kid.

"How's business, Dad? Everything churning right along on Wall Street?"

"Oh, fine, fine."

"My," said my mother, "you people still have snow up here. Back home in Greenwich, the daffodils are out and the trees are starting to blossom. Wilma Henderson, at garden club yesterday, predicted this would be a banner year for the dogwoods."

"Nifty," I said.

My parents caught me eyeing the pair of overloaded shopping bags they had carried up from the car. One of the bags said Saks Fifth Avenue. The other had come from Lord & Taylor.

"Oh," my mother said, "I do hope you won't think us too forward, Mr. Kirk, but I had Luroleen toss a few snacks in. Just in case Collin missed some of his favorites."

Blowing my cool, I made almost a leaping dive at the bags.

Dad snorted. "Greedy as ever."

"That's me," I admitted, tearing into a package that turned out to be one of Luroleen's king-size fruitcakes. Grabbing some plates, I used the hunting knife to slice the cake into five healthy portions. Tool snapped up her share with one famished bite.

Sabbath Kirk ate. So did I, watching him devour the fruitcake and hearing him tell Mom how tasty it was. Neither my father nor my mother ate even one bite. They just stared at how Tool and Mr. Kirk and I finished ours before the two of them could even begin.

"Aren't you hungry?" I asked.

"Not terribly," Mom said. "Your father and I lunched in Middlebury. My, such a sumptuous buffet they have at the Middlebury Inn. Collin, you and Mr. Kirk must go there sometime and . . ." She stopped talking.

I wanted to hug her. Mom didn't know. Yet she sensed something about which she was not eager to inquire. She was aware of how far away she was from Greenwich, Connecticut.

Dad said, "We won't pop in on you fellows again like this, I promise. We're probably just in the way."

"I made him come." Mother smiled at me and at Mr. Kirk. "I just *had* to see for myself what was happening with Collin." She spotted something once again on the floor. A hen feather.

"See?" Dad nodded. "I told you he'd be fine. Every boy ought to have an opportunity like this. Plenty of fresh air and woods to hike around in. And chores to be done."

"Mr. Kirk and I are okay," I said. "You don't need to worry about us anymore. And we have Tool to keep us company."

"So I see," Mom said. Rising from the cot, she stretched out a hand to pet Tool. "Nice doggy." Ears back, Tool bared her teeth and snarled. My mother retreated and looked at her hand.

"Oh, before I forget," I said, "when you get home, give my love to Winnie. And please tell Luroleen thank you for all the chow. I really appreciate it."

"Are you eating well here?"

"Sure. We're okay."

"Your hair," my mother said. "It looks as though it hasn't been combed since I saw you last."

I smiled. "Guess it hasn't."

"Good," said Dad.

29

I hiked with them down to the Lincoln.

"Now," said Mom, hugging me hard, "you're *sure* you'll be all right up here?"

"Of course he will." Dad grunted. "After all, he's got Mr. Kirk to look after him and wipe his nose."

"Remember," my mother said, "you have all that food we brought, so please don't let it go to waste. Not with prices the way they are. You'll find two quarts of eggnog, boiled ham, several big packets of cheese, and some crackers. Yes, and half a dozen pears."

I smiled at her. "No hors d'oeuvres?"

"No way," Dad shot back. "You're not up here to stuff your gullet with fancy food."

Smiling at my father, I said, "I guess you're right, Dad. I'm not."

"To tell you the truth, son, when I dropped you here, I worried how you'd do."

"I'm doing it."

"And I honestly expected that as soon as you saw

your mother and me, you'd start whimpering to come home."

"Not yet. I'll tough it out."

"Good." He squeezed my hand. "I'm proud of you. You're a different boy, Collin." His voice softened. "Not the same kid you were a few weeks ago. Must be all the fun you're having."

I shrugged. "Must be."

My mother hugged me again. "Collin, *do* promise me just one thing."

"Sure. You name it."

"Please don't go *near* that *dreadful* dog."

"I won't, Mom. And if I do, I give you my word I won't hurt her."

Mother let out a sigh as she climbed in the car. "You'll never change, Collin. Nothing to you is serious."

"Nope," I said. "Nary a thing. Remember, say hi to Luroleen for me, and ask her not to mess up my room, because I just might come home someday. And say hi to Grandfather. Tell him I miss him."

Dad started the car. "Hang in there, son."

"I'll come home when I'm ready. So long. And thanks for coming to see us."

"Good-bye, dear." Mom waved to me.

I watched the Lincoln turn around and grind down the dirt road, hearing its engine fade into nothing but the chirp of chickadees.

Back at the cabin, Mr. Kirk was up and out of his rocker, stirring into the Lord & Taylor bag of goodies.

"You got good folks, boy."

"I know."

"You're right precious to the both of 'em."

"I'm glad about that." I opened a hunk of orange cheddar cheese. "Because they're precious to me. I just never knew how much."

"You never told 'em all ya done."

"No."

"How come?"

I answered him with a mouthful of cheese. "I didn't feel the need to tell them. Doing it was enough."

Sabbath Kirk punched my arm. "That's my Collie."

I grinned at him. "You know, Mr. Kirk, I've never had a nickname before. Guys I went to school with were called J.P. and Jimbo and Corky. But nobody seemed to care enough to give *me* a nickname."

"Had me a collie dog once. Years back, when I was farming. I never named her like I done for Tool. Just called her Collie."

"I bet she was a real neat dog."

"That she be. Or was. When I dug her grave, it dang near busted up my heart. She was a beauty of an animal. With spirit and gumption—like you, boy."

"Oh, shut up and eat your cheese."

The old man grinned, his upper lip yellow with egg froth. We polished off one of the quarts of eggnog, all of one cheese, and then ate the two slices of fruit-cake that Mom and Dad had left untouched on their plates.

"Mr. Kirk, it's been one whale of a month."

"Dang if it ain't." Limping over to the sink, he sorted through one of his countless old coffee cans. Returning, he held out his fist. "Here ya go."

"What is it?"

"You'll see."

I uncrumpled what had been hiding in his hand. A dollar bill. Having totally forgotten our contract that he would pay me a dollar a month, I guess my mouth fell open.

"Take it, boy. And squirrel it away. Because you more 'n earned it."

Holding the bill, I said, "I more 'n did. And I'll always keep it. This is the most important buck I'll ever earn."

I ordered Mr. Kirk to take a late afternoon nap on his cot, while I carefully unloaded all the food and made sure it would keep fresh, packing the eggnog in snow. Outside it was thawing. April was softening at last, promising May.

I couldn't resist the pears. The first went down so easily that I gobbled up another. There is something about a juicy yellow pear that beats a meal of bacon grease.

Tomorrow, I vowed, I would take Tool and go hunting. Maybe the old man might want to tag along, but I'd warn him not to get underfoot. Tool and I could manage alone. I'd shoot it, clean it, and cook it —even if it was Loomis Broom.

Mr. Kirk awakened, and we ate again, with Tool.

She went outside and scampered in circles. To see her finally prance was some sight. I took an empty bucket and went with her as far as the spring, where the cool water bubbled up from its rock bed among ferns. Leaning down, I drank a long cold lap of Vermont water. So did the dog.

Then Tool ran off, dancing her freedom like a pup.

The ripples in the spring quieted, and I blinked down at my own face. It was a sight I hadn't seen for weeks. I looked blankly at Collin Richardson Pepper. The face looked the same, but I thought, I'm not the same person. Nor would I ever be again. There was too much to do.

I smiled at the shimmering face, and it smiled back. "So long forever, candy-ass," I said.

And, I thought, at last I know who I am. Sometime soon, I'll have a chat with Grandfather. Maybe about becoming a doctor. But not yet. I won't leave Mr. Kirk and Tool until I'm certain they can fend without me.

Then it hit me—my timetable. I'd stay up here until August, when the War Head would flame once more, heading south. Telling me to do likewise, head south, back home to my folks and to school. I'd stay five months and go home with five bucks in my pocket, well earned. I'd go with the War Head.

Whistling, my free arm extended for balance, I returned with my bucket of fresh water, taking it to the sink. I made sure there was water in the teakettle that slept on the Acme American.

The old man was up again, and there was no holding him down. "Come on, Collie."

"Where to?"

"Outside. I'm going to stretch my pins before they buckle up and give. Best I work out the kinks."

I bundled him into his coat, kept on mine, and we ventured out into the late April evening. Brown holes were thawing in the wet snow. The old man leaned into the trunk of a sturdy pine, his arms embracing it all.

"We done her, Collie."

"So we did." I put my hand on his shoulder.

He turned. "Thank you, boy. Whatever life I got left, I hereby do thank you for the all of it. Every dang lick."

"Mr. Kirk—thanks for mine."

"We sure are a perditious pair, ain't we?"

I made a face at him. "Yup. That we be."

The old man pointed upward to the shelf of gray granite. "Climb up, boy."

"Now?"

He nodded. "Hasten, before it's too late."

In seconds, I was atop the big rocks, looking westward, now knowing why he wanted me up here. To the west, the pink-and-lavender sunset sharpened downward to focus into the fire of the War Head.

"Tell me what you see, boy," the old man yelled up. "I'll picture her from down here. Pity I need a young punk to do my lookin' for me."

"Sir, I see a warrior. An old warrior asleep on his

mountain." My words weren't easy to say. "And he's the meanest old devil that ever got hatched."

From below, Sabbath Kirk waved his hat at me. "Tell me, Collie. Is he an old dead warrior yet?"

"No, sir. He's still alive."